HACKING MR. CEO

BILLIONAIRE HEISTS #3

ANNA HACKETT

Hacking Mr. CEO

Published by Anna Hackett

Copyright 2021 by Anna Hackett

Cover by RBA Designs

Cover image by Wander Aguiar

Edits by Tanya Saari

ISBN (ebook): 978-1-922414-33-5

ISBN (paperback): 978-1-922414-34-2

WHAT READERS ARE SAYING ABOUT
ANNA'S ACTION ROMANCE

The Investigator and The Troubleshooter -
Romantic Book of the Year (Ruby) finalists
2021

Heart of Eon - Romantic Book of the Year
(Ruby) winner 2020

Cyborg - PRISM Award Winner 2019

Edge of Eon and Mission: Her Protection -
Romantic Book of the Year (Ruby) finalists
2019

Unfathomed and Unmapped - Romantic Book
of the Year (Ruby) finalists 2018

Unexplored – Romantic Book of the Year
(Ruby) Novella Winner 2017

Return to Dark Earth – One of Library Journal's Best E-Original Books for 2015 and two-time SFR Galaxy Awards winner

At Star's End – One of Library Journal's Best E-Original Romances for 2014

The Phoenix Adventures – SFR Galaxy Award Winner for Most Fun New Series and "Why Isn't This a Movie?" Series

Beneath a Trojan Moon – SFR Galaxy Award Winner and RWAus Ella Award Winner

Hell Squad – SFR Galaxy Award for best Post-Apocalypse for Readers who don't like Post-Apocalypse

"Action, danger, aliens, romance – yup, it's another great book from Anna Hackett!" – Book Gannet Reviews, review of *Hell Squad: Marcus*

Sign up for my VIP mailing list and get your *free box set* containing three action-packed romances.

Visit here to get started: www.annahackett.com

ROGUE ANGEL

Remi

"Oh, you think you can keep me out? Not today."
My fingers danced over my keyboard. It glowed,
each keystroke near soundless. I'd paid a small fortune for
the keyboard and laptop.

They were my babies.

I'd already mapped the target system. Their cybersecurity was good, but not great. I knew I had tripped some
alarm, so they were aware I was poking around.

"But no one can stop the Rogue Angel." With a smile,
I stared at the glowing screen, analyzing the code. I
tapped in a command.

Woot. I was in.

I wiggled my butt in my chair. *Time to finish this.*

I zoomed through the system, found the file I needed,
and made a copy.

Time to go.

I left my signature image behind—glowing, blue angel wings made of computer code.

Smiling, I sat back and flexed my hands. Then I polished my nails on my shirt, and blew on them. I was a hacker, so I kept my nails short and neat, but I loved painting them. They were currently bright, eye-searing yellow.

Next, I opened up a new window and made a call.

My boss appeared on-screen.

I took a second to appreciate the view—Killian Hawke deserved a second or two of appreciation.

The man always made me think of a sharp blade, honed to precision. He was lean, had a hawkish face, black hair, black eyes. Those eyes were sharp and missed nothing. He wore a black suit even though it was Sunday —I'd never seen him in anything else. Even across the computer screen, he radiated a predatory danger that made my hindbrain sit very, very still.

"Done," I said. "Check your inbox."

The head of Sentinel Security glanced to his left, then nodded.

"Well done, Remi. Impressive, as always."

Damn, the man had the sexiest voice. Like warm, melted chocolate with a dash of spice. It totally didn't go with the sleek, dangerous persona.

"Our client will be very happy," Killian said.

"Happy that I hacked them?"

"Happy they know their vulnerabilities, and how Sentinel Security can help plug them."

And pay Killian a bazillion dollars for his trouble.

Sentinel did all kinds of security. I knew Killian had a

private army of ex-military badasses, but he also specialized in cybersecurity. I'd been working for Sentinel for several years. Companies hired me to test their systems and improve their security. It was a sweet deal. I used my special skills, and got a paycheck at the end of each month.

"I'll email you your next job, Remi." The faintest tilt of Killian's lips. "Or should I say, Rogue Angel?"

I grinned. "You aren't supposed to know my secret persona."

"I'm in security, remember?"

"Bye, Bossman."

I ended the chat, closed my laptop, then glanced at my watch. The kids would be home from school soon, and my stomach rumbled. Mmm, I could do with some of Mama's cookies.

I strode across my loft space. It wasn't big, but it was mine. It had an industrial vibe, with my bed in one corner, shrouded by gauzy curtains. A tiny kitchenette that I barely used sat in another corner, a doorway led into my compact bathroom, and an open-plan living area where my desk took prime position against the far wall.

My gaze snagged on a picture above the desk.

I got a little shiver every time I saw it. It was of an angel warrior, coming in to land on the battlefield. I had a thing for angels. His huge, white wings were outspread, sword in hand, boots about to touch the ground. His body was mostly in shadow, but that didn't hide the power of his musculature, or the hint of a rugged face.

Wrinkling my nose, I sighed. I wished they made men like that in real life.

I headed down the stairs, my boots thunking on the metal treads.

Noise assaulted me. There was some tool whirring close by, and I also got a hit of grease, gas, and exhaust.

My loft was above my foster brother's auto shop. At the bottom of the stairs, I swiveled and saw three cars in various states of repair—one parked with the hood open, one hooked up to some machine, and another one up on the hoist, with a mechanic underneath.

I recognized Steve's lean body, and baggy, grimy jeans. He was busy, and the guy that worked for him was away on vacation, so I guess that was why he was working on a Sunday. I headed out the open front doors.

Brr. It was a cold, gloomy day in Brooklyn. I wrapped my arms around myself. I should've grabbed my jacket, but thankfully I wasn't going far.

I went next door to the two-story, brick house and opened the gate. The metal screeched.

The house had a downstairs basement apartment, where Steve lived with his four-year-old daughter, Kaylee. I jogged up the steps to the main house and opened the door.

"Hello!"

"We're back here," a female voice said.

I found Mama Alma in the kitchen. Of course, where else would she be? Kaylee was on the floor having a tea party with her dolls and bears.

"Remi!" The little blonde princess leaped up and ran at me. I caught her, and she wrapped her arms and legs around me. I breathed in her apple-scented shampoo.

"Hey, KayKay. You being good for Mama?"

Kaylee smiled and nodded. Then she wriggled and I let her down to return to her tea party guests.

Mama smiled, and I walked over to press a kiss to her dark, papery cheek.

She smelled like home. For the first eight years of my life, I hadn't known what that word meant. Then angels had smiled on me, and sent an angry little girl to this foster home run by Mama.

She'd owned this house in Sunset Park, Brooklyn for years. The small warehouse next door had been her husband's. Unable to have kids of their own, they'd become foster parents. Big Mike died the year before I'd arrived, but Alma hadn't stopped opening her home.

And some of us hadn't really left. I'd be twenty-seven on my next birthday, and I hadn't gone far. Steve had been one of Mama's first foster kids. Kaylee was Steve's daughter, but Mama still had three kids with her—two boys, aged nine and ten, and a teenaged girl.

"I'll pour us some tea," Mama said.

I dropped into the chair at the rickety table. The kitchen hadn't changed in decades. "I'd prefer a shot of bourbon to celebrate. I just finished a job."

Mama made a sound in her throat. "No bourbon in this house."

I snatched a cookie off the plate on the table. *Mmm.* Chocolate chip, my favorite.

She set a teacup in front of me. Mama loved collecting flowery, delicate cups from flea markets. None of them matched.

Like my family, Mama always told me.

As I finished my cookie, I studied Mama—she looked

tired, and her face was drawn. I frowned. Mama always said that she was a mix of the best—African-American, a dash of Hispanic, and some hardy Irish stock.

I think that's why I'd liked her on sight—I was a mix, too. Mostly Hispanic, although I had no idea who my parents were. I probably had an African-American ancestor somewhere in the tree as well, and some other things—who knew what—dashed in.

Mama had beautiful, dark-brown skin, and tightly coiled, black hair. She was also two inches taller than me.

I sighed and sipped my tea. I was curvy and petite, aka short, at five feet—okay, *almost* five feet. And I had hips, a butt, and boobs. My dark-brown hair got a few golden streaks in the summer, more so if I actually made it out in the sun.

"You okay, Mama?"

"Fine, child, fine." She didn't meet my gaze.

My heart sank. She was lying. Mama never lied. Sometimes she chose not to answer, but she never lied.

"Mama?" I pressed my hand to hers. *When had it gotten so frail?*

She looked away, down at Kaylee. That's when I noticed the paperwork on the table.

I grabbed it.

"Remina, no—"

I scanned it. It was a letter from a doctor. I saw the words and my chest locked.

Looking up at the woman who'd been my mother, father, friend, and savior, I shook my head. "Brain tumor?" My words were a harsh whisper.

Mama pressed her lips together and nodded.

No. *No.* Mama was the glue in our little world. I looked at Kaylee, swallowed, then met Mama's dark gaze.

"So, what's the treatment? Chemo?" My stomach lurched at the thought, but whatever we had to do to get her well, we'd do it.

"It's..." Mama cleared her throat. "The doctor said chemo won't help."

"What?" Panic was slick and ugly in my throat. "So, what, then?"

"Nothing, my child."

Nothing. I looked at the letter blankly and saw what it said. "Six months?"

Mama shifted in her chair, her eyes covered with a sheen of tears. "No one can say for sure. The Lord always has a plan."

"Screw that." I stood up and saw Kaylee jerk in surprise. "Sorry, Kaylee." I snatched up another sheet of paper, and Mama tried to grab it. I sucked in a breath. "There's an operation."

Mama straightened. "It's experimental, Remi. There's no guarantee it would work." A pause. "And it's very expensive."

I looked down. When I saw the dollar amount, it felt like my feet had fallen through the floor. I gripped the edge of the table.

"Mama—"

The front door slammed, followed by the sound of running feet and young voices.

"Mama! We're home from the park."

Two boys raced in, dumping their backpacks on the floor. Charlie, who had a sturdy body, a mop of red hair, and freckles. Jamal followed one step behind. He was skinny, dark-skinned, and had a shy smile. The two were thick as thieves.

"Charlie. Jami," Kaylee called.

The boys hugged Mama, me, then Kaylee.

Naomi came in at a slower pace. At fifteen, she was too old to run and play like the kids, and she was surgically attached to her phone. She did well at school, stayed out of trouble, and loved to cook and bake.

"Mama, I'm making cookies," Naomi said.

"I already did, child."

"I see Remi's been into them. We'll need more."

I poked my tongue out. Naomi was five foot seven—all the height that I'd once dreamed about.

"I have to run." I hugged Mama, a little harder than usual. "We'll talk later. Everything will be okay."

"I love you, Remi Solano."

"I love you, too." I fought to keep my shit together and headed back to my loft. I managed to avoid Steve.

Dropping into my desk chair, I sat in front of my laptop, staring blankly at the wall. I thought of the kids, Steve and Kaylee, me.

We *couldn't* lose Mama.

It was so unfair. My face twisted. She'd given *so* much. Was so loving and selfless. I wanted to scream, or throw something.

Without stopping to think, I opened my laptop. I tapped quickly, heading into a dark part of the Web.

I was a white-hat hacker. I legally hacked to test client systems. White hats were usually employed by the government or security companies.

Okay, I was a white-hat hacker with a dash of gray. Gray hats had no agenda, and hacked for fun.

Black-hat hackers on the other hand...

My stomach coiled. I left a note on a black-hat message board.

Rogue Angel available.

I couldn't let Mama die.

Mav

Maverick Rivera finished tying his bowtie and shrugged into his tuxedo jacket.

He headed for the door, sending one last glance at the naked woman lying facedown in the bed, sound asleep.

He didn't leave his number. He never did. He'd met her in the bar downstairs. He only hooked up with women who wanted exactly what he did—a few hours of no-strings attached sex.

Heading out of the hotel room, he made his way down to the ballroom.

He scowled at the din of the crowd.

Another damn party to go to.

This shindig was for some veterans' charity his friend Liam supported. Mav would prefer to be home with a glass of scotch, or in his lab. Still, as his friends liked to remind him, he had to be social sometimes, and at least this one was for a good cause.

He stepped into the ballroom. It looked like half of New York society was here.

The room was bathed in golden light. Huge, gold candelabras adorned the circular tables.

Outside, snow was falling. He scanned the space, looking for his two best friends. Usually, the three of them would sample the scotch, make a donation, and avoid the society mamas out to marry their daughters off to billionaires.

But things had changed recently.

His gut clenched, and he nabbed a server to order a scotch on the rocks. "Macallan, if you have it."

The man nodded. "Right away, sir."

When Mav turned back, he spotted Zane on the dance floor. The King of Wall Street was smiling down at the woman he held tight in his arms. Monroe wore a long, silver dress that sparkled, her long, black hair loose over her shoulders.

Mav had met Zane Roth and Liam Kensington at college. They'd all become friends, brothers. Each of them had gone on to make their fortunes: Zane in finance, Liam in property and development, and Mav in tech.

Unfortunately, that also painted targets on their backs.

Another couple whizzed past, laughing with Zane and Monroe.

Liam had some smooth moves on the dance floor. He came from money—he could dance, hobnob with perfect manners, and wore a tux like he'd been born in one.

He held his new girlfriend, and the love of his life, tucked against him. Aspen's platinum-blonde hair was up tonight, leaving her shoulders bare. She wore a column of black that hugged her athletic body, and flared out at her knees. Liam's tailor was having a grand time dressing the woman.

Yeah, the billionaire bachelors of New York were no more. There was only him now, and he'd never get married.

"Your drink, sir."

He lifted his chin at the server, and accepted his drink.

Mav had long-ago learned that trusting a woman was a fool's game. They wanted all kinds of things, but mostly they wanted money.

He glanced at his friends and their women. He'd had his doubts about Monroe and Aspen at first—but it hadn't taken him long to like them. And what they brought to his friends.

The couples were in love. Mav sipped his scotch again, grudgingly admitting that they were the exception that proved the rule.

Love was for idiots.

He had Hannah to thank for that lesson.

His final year of college, he'd met a smart, pretty, girl-next-door. She'd been blonde, blue-eyed, tall and slim. She'd fallen for him, and he'd fallen for her. In truth, she'd fallen for his first billion dollars.

He'd just sold his first invention—a new computer chip. Money had been about to come pouring in, and there'd been articles about him.

He'd never suspected Hannah wasn't the real deal. That pretty face, the earnest smile, the good sex. Fuck, he'd bought her flowers. He tossed back the rest of his drink.

Ancient fucking history.

He should be thanking Hannah. She'd taught him a valuable lesson.

"Mav." The dark-haired Zane appeared and slapped Mav's back. Monroe leaned in and kissed his cheek.

"Hey," Mav said.

"The great man emerges from his Batcave," a female voice drawled.

He shot Aspen a scowl, and the private investigator just smiled. Liam kept an arm around her and reached out to shake Mav's hand.

They were both healing up well after being trapped in a burning warehouse. Liam and Aspen had been embroiled in some trouble recently.

"Hey, any luck stopping those hacks on Rivera Tech?" Liam asked.

Last week, the system at Rivera Tech had been hammered by a string of hacking attempts. It lasted for a few days, and kept Mav and his team busy. Then it had stopped.

The hackers had either given up, or they'd hired someone better.

"They stopped. I've been busy increasing system security since then," Mav said. "How are things with you?"

"Well, Aspen's sisters text me at least twice a day, giddy about having her apartment to themselves," Liam said.

Aspen snagged a glass of champagne from a server.

"Hey, I have a multi-million-dollar penthouse to call home now. I'm not complaining. I do miss Mrs. Kerber, though. My old neighbor. I've asked Juno and Briar to help her if her bird, Skittles, escapes again."

And there it was. Aspen was good, down to her bones.

"And," Liam said. "My personal PI managed to track down the girls in the photographs with my father." The man's lip curled.

Mav's fingers tightened on his glass. Liam hated his father. The elder Kensington was an asshole with a predilection for underage, teenage girls. That, mixed in with some white-collar criminals and a blackmail attempt, was how Aspen and Liam had met.

Aspen leaned into her man. "One of the girls has agreed to press charges."

Liam's smile was grim. "My father will finally pay for his crimes."

Mav lifted his glass. "I'll drink to that."

"Well, my billionaire boyfriend is driving me *nuts*," Monroe declared, in an obvious attempt to lighten the mood.

Zane rolled his eyes.

Mav raised a brow. "He can be pretty annoying at times."

Now Zane shot Mav a narrow look.

"He wants to invest in Lady Locksmith and help me expand the stores," Monroe said.

Aspen swiveled. "And that's a bad thing?"

Liam nodded. "Sounds like a good investment, to me."

Monroe, daughter of a career thief, ran a locksmith shop, specializing in providing female locksmiths to the women of New York. She was also a pro at cracking a safe, which was how she'd met Zane—when she'd cracked his.

"I know, but it's mine." Monroe's nose wrinkled. "He owns the rest of New York."

Zane tugged her close. "I just want you happy."

She cupped his cheek. "I am happy."

Mav had to look away. The song changed.

"Oh, I *love* this one," Monroe said. "Come on. We're dancing."

Liam groaned. "Chandler here has two left feet."

His woman elbowed him. "You were warned."

"But for the chance to hold you in my arms, darling, it's worth the pain."

The couples headed off and Mav felt... It sure as hell wasn't envy. *Relief.* Yeah, he was too smart to get tangled up with that.

"Maverick Rivera," a voice drawled.

He turned and hid a grimace. *Oh, no.*

Mrs. Randolph, one of New York's most prominent socialites, bore down on him.

"I want to introduce you to my *lovely* daughter." The woman tilted her coiffed head.

Mav saw the tall, slim blonde nearby. She smiled coyly at him.

"No," he growled.

Mrs. Randolph missed a step and blinked. She probably didn't hear that word often. "Well, I think there's no harm in—"

"No." Mav held up his empty glass. "I need a drink. Have a nice evening."

He headed to the bar.

Yeah, Hannah had taught him a lesson, and his heart was too scarred to ever let anyone in again.

He loved his family.

He loved Zane and Liam, and now their women.

But Mav was never, ever falling in love again.

He leaned against the bar. "Scotch. A double."

2

FORT KNOX

Remi

I stared at the screen, my gut churning. The cursor blinked at me.

I had a job from the black-hat board.

There was a crash from the next room.

"*Hey*," I called out. "Don't break anything."

"Sorry, Remi," Charlie chimed. "It was an accident."

Sure, it was. I sat at the kitchen table, and Mama was taking a nap. The kids were back from school, and I'd offered to look after them for a bit. She'd looked so tired. I nibbled on my bottom lip. I knew Charlie and Jamal were wrestling.

Naomi was humming behind me as she made a cake. She had air pods in her ears, and was dancing a little as she mixed and stirred.

Jamal streaked through the kitchen, laughing, followed by a determined-looking Charlie. A few seconds later, a giggling Kaylee followed, trying to keep up with the boys.

It felt like a rock lodged in my throat.

If Mama didn't make it...

I dropped my head into my hands. The job waiting for me itched. I've never broken the law before. Okay, one time I'd shoplifted, because Marianne Anderson had dared me. I'd taken a tube of lip-gloss and a packet of chewing gum. When Mama found out, she'd marched me down to the store to return them and apologize. I'd also done my fair share of hacking, which wasn't strictly legal, but I'd never stolen or compromised anything.

Shit, if Mama knew what I was considering, she'd freak.

The front door opened, and I heard heavy footsteps. I closed the lid on my laptop.

Steve came in. He wore a black T-shirt with Steve's Auto embroidered on it, and he had a greasy rag hanging from the back pocket of his jeans.

"Hey," he said.

"Hi."

Kaylee rushed in. "Daddy!"

Steve hugged his daughter tight. "How's my best girl?"

My heart melted. He was such a good dad. His girl-friend had run off when Kaylee was two. A toddler had put a real crimp in Crystal's partying. I'd never liked her. Steve had been a single dad ever since. He'd told me numerous times that he couldn't do it without Mama.

More weight settled on my shoulders.

Maybe I didn't have to take this black-hat job. Maybe

I could work my tail off for Killian, and Steve could pitch in, and I could take out a loan or something.

Steve dropped heavily into the chair across from me, and scraped a hand over his face.

Shit, did he know about Mama?

"Everything okay?" I asked.

He met my gaze. "Not yet. But I'll get there." He released a long breath. "I've had a few clients who haven't paid recently. They're having cash flow problems."

"*What*?" I leaned forward. "Then they don't get you to do work, if they don't have the money to pay for it."

"Cool it, Remi. They're guys I know. They're going through bad times. One's filing for bankruptcy." He sighed. "Things will just be tight for a little bit, that's all."

God. I stared blindly at the floor. He couldn't help with medical costs, then. And if Mama wasn't around to take care of Kaylee, he'd have to pay someone.

"Hey, I've got work to do before dinner. You got the kids?"

Steve waved a hand. "Go."

I scooped up my laptop and raced back to my loft. All the way, I tried to swallow the bad taste in my mouth, but I thought of Mama, Steve and Kaylee, the kids...

And me.

A world without Mama Alma wasn't one I could picture.

I had to protect my family, the same way Mama had protected me. With grim determination, I sat at the desk in my loft and opened my laptop.

Opening the browser, I went to the black-hat board. It filled the screen.

I clicked on the job.

Good day, Rogue Angel. Your reputation precedes you. I have a job that only someone of your caliber could handle.

"Yeah, yeah, flattery will get you nowhere."

The payment for the job is one million dollars.

I gasped. Holy cow, a *million* bucks. I took a few steadying breaths. That was enough to get Mama her treatment. I gripped the arms of my chair. I saw Kaylee had stuck some Angel stickers on them. I scratched my nail on the glittery surface.

I'd do anything for my family.

I clicked the next page.

The job is to hack into Rivera Tech, and copy all files referring to the Calix Project.

Oh. *Hell.*

Rivera Tech.

One of the biggest tech companies on the planet. Hell, my laptop was Rivera Tech.

I groaned. If anyone would have top-grade security, it would be Maverick Rivera, billionaire CEO owner of Rivera Tech.

I stared at the screen and pulled up a search. I typed in his name.

A picture popped up and my heart did a little bounce. *Likey, likey.*

I snorted. *Yeah, yeah, so does every other woman in New York City.*

He was big—tall, broad shoulders. The guy had to work out, because I knew for a fact sitting behind a computer all day didn't make you look like that. He was

ANNA HACKETT

handsome in a rugged, rough kind of way. He had dark-bronze skin, dark-brown eyes, and stubble across a hard jaw. I was a sucker for stubble. For some reason, instead of sitting at a computer, I pictured him holding a sword, not a keyboard.

A headache bloomed behind my left eye, and I rubbed my temple. Then I opened the drawer and grabbed some gum. I chewed, hoping it would ease my anxiety.

Dammit, Rivera Tech was renowned for killer security. Hell, Rivera had invented half the stuff used on every computer today.

But no system was unbeatable. I thought of Mama, then tapped on my keyboard.

I'll do it.

There. Done.

A message popped up almost instantly.

Very well. You have one week.

I closed my eyes. *What had I gotten myself into?*

I straightened and thought of Mama.

Okay. I needed to map out Rivera's network and search for vulnerabilities. Find all the strengths and weaknesses of his system. I tapped my foot on the floor. I knew some gray-hat hacker friends, and surely someone would've tried to crack Rivera Tech before. They could have valuable intel for me.

I considered contacting my online hacker friend, Wesley. We'd met two years ago online. He was pure geek to the bone and lived in his mother's basement. She cooked for him and did all his laundry.

But lately, he kept asking me out. Okay, he'd asked

me out about four-hundred times. The man couldn't take a hint and I was running out of ways to tell him I wasn't interested without hurting him. No, I wouldn't call Wes.

I'd send a few emails in a little bit, but right now, I could do a little flyby.

I wiggled my fingers, took a second to admire my nails, and then pulled up a window. I tapped in a command and opened a little program I'd created myself.

Okay, time to dance.

I didn't hammer the Rivera Tech system. I danced along the edges. I sent out a few pings. Active reconnaissance involved interacting with a target. It gave more accurate information, but it came with the increased risk of getting caught by a firewall or network security.

Crap. I studied the data.

Crap. Crap. Crap on a stick.

Rivera's system was pure beauty.

Fort Knox.

I gnawed on my lip. I wanted to take a closer look. I tapped furiously.

As I looked, my belly tied into knots.

This would be no walk in the park. I was good, but what I was seeing may take me longer than a week to crack.

The guy had alarms everywhere. He had back up security on his backups.

"Man, someone's a little paranoid."

It made sense. Rivera was a tech God. He'd have loads of important stuff on the system. And I suspected there were people who'd pay loads to get their hands on his designs. A little corporate espionage.

My chest locked. Probably like my new mystery employer.

I hated not knowing who the job was for. Or what I was handing over exactly.

No turning back now.

I heard a ping and froze. I scanned the screen.

Oh, no. *No, no, no.*

My fingers blurred as I typed. *Fuck.* I'd set off an alarm.

It's okay. I wasn't deep in the system, just on the outer layers. Besides, I was Rogue Angel. No one would be good enough to catch me.

My pulse slowed, and a sense of calm descended, along with the bite of excitement.

Yes, going somewhere you shouldn't felt just a little exhilarating.

I'd take a look around a little more, clear my tracks, then disappear for now.

And no doubt leave the Rivera Tech security geeks scratching their heads.

Mav

He hammered the punching bag—left, right, knee, hook, kick.

Mav's grunts and the slap of flesh on the bag filled the gym.

With a final spin, he slammed a hard roundhouse kick into the bag, sending it swinging.

Sucking in air, he pressed his hands to his knees. Sweat made his workout gear stick to his skin. He worked out a few times a week with Liam, Zane, and their tough, crusty trainer Simeon. The guy was a Krav Maga expert and a hard task master.

Mav and his friends knew early on that they didn't want to be trailed by security or bodyguards 24/7, so they'd made a pact to learn how to defend themselves. Mav also worked out here at home, in his decked-out home gym. He liked the challenge of pushing himself, lifting weights, building strength. He also liked running on the treadmill, or punching the shit out of the punching bag. It helped clear his head.

Most of all, he loved computers and inventing new, exciting tech that solved problems. He liked nothing more than losing himself in designing a new program, or fiddling around in his lab.

Unfortunately, bringing all that to market meant meetings, business shit, financials, interviews, and people.

Yeah, he could do without the people bit.

Mav had always been the big, quiet kid growing up. He'd always felt awkward and out of place.

Until his dad had brought home an old, secondhand PC. And then Mav had met his computer studies teacher in high school. Mr. Walker was a total geek, and he'd introduced Mav to coding.

Mav had found the place where everything flowed and made sense.

His phone pinged.

Frowning, he walked to the bench against the far

wall. He took a sip of water as he unlocked the new Rivera Tech prototype phone with a retinal scan.

A glowing-red notification filled the screen.

Someone had triggered an alarm on the Rivera Tech system.

Fucking hackers.

Phone in hand, he strode out of the gym and down the hall to his office. Aspen liked calling it the Batcave. It had dark-gray walls, and a long, sleek desk filled with multiple screens. He kept the blinds closed.

He dropped into his chair and swiveled. The screens flared to life.

"Good evening, Maverick," a voice similar to the computer on *Star Trek* said.

"Open program Delta six."

"Opening."

He pulled a sleek keyboard closer and got to work.

A hacker friend of Monroe's had gotten into his system recently, while helping her out. Mav now had Rollo on the payroll. They'd souped-up the security system a lot, and they had a lot more planned.

He also had a team of cybersecurity experts, but anyone who got too far, he liked to deal with himself.

He eyed the hacker's trail.

Hmm, they were just doing a flyby. Skimming the outer edges and taking a peek. No doubt mapping the network to find any vulnerabilities to exploit. Then they'd plan an assault and return later.

Not happening. Mav followed the hacker. He set up a secondary program to trace the asshole.

The hacker stopped and started clearing their tracks.

Yeah, the big, bad wolf is on to you. Mav opened a chat window directly to the hacker.

Get the fuck out, asshole.

> *Well, you don't mince words, do you?*

Maverick raised his eyebrows. Any other hacker would be scrambling to get away.

> *I'm not hurting anything. Just taking a look.*

Mav shook his head at the arrogance. Like the asshole was just out for a stroll.

Get gone, or you'll regret it.

He glanced at the tracking program. The hacker was definitely in the USA. He watched the data tick by as it tried to find where. Then he'd sic the FBI onto them.

> *Ooh, I'm shaking in my boots.*

Mav scowled. Shit, maybe he'd gotten used to people doing what he asked instantly. Not many people ever disagreed with him, or said no. He typed.

What do you want?

> *Nothing right now.*

> *You think I don't recognize network mapping when I see it?*

You can't see me, but I'm fluttering my lashes, all innocent-like.

He snorted. Shit, a funny hacker. He stilled. Something about the wording gave off a feminine vibe.

He was certain his hacker was a woman.

So, you work for Rivera Tech security? I didn't think Maverick Rivera would hire such chatty, friendly guys like you.

Mav glanced at the tracking program. She was on the East Coast.

You'd be surprised at what Maverick Rivera does.

No, I don't think so. That big, broody billionaire is either inventing
a new gazillion-dollar gadget, or buying a new yacht.

A laugh burst out of him. It sounded a little rusty.

I don't own a yacht. I just hire one when the mood strikes.

There was no response. He stared at the blinking cursor.

You're Maverick Rivera?

Yes. And who are you?

Wouldn't you like to know?

Suddenly, he really did. He was actually having fun.
Why are you cruising my system, mystery girl?

How do you know I'm a girl?

I can tell.

No, you can't. I'm a middle-aged, Ukrainian hacker called Sergei.

Mav snorted.
Nope.
He looked at the other screen, and his pulse leaped. She was in New York.

Okay, maybe I'm a thirteen-year-old, Russian hacker called Nikolai.

Mav swallowed another laugh.
Not buying it. So why are you here?
There was a long pause, and for a second, he thought she'd left.

I don't want to be, believe me.

He frowned.

Well, I have to go.

No.
Shit, was he crazy? He didn't need her in his fucking

system. She was only a few layers in, but he could already tell she was good.

I know you're trying to track me.

No, I'm not.

Wow, you're a bad liar, even online.

The tracker zoomed in and his pulse spiked. She was in New York City.

Then the screen flickered and the tracker program froze.

What the hell? He tapped furiously.

Suddenly, the tracker was replaced by an image of two glowing-blue angel wings, made of computer code.

Nice try, Maverick Rivera.

He ground his teeth together. She was good. She was very good.

If you come back, I will hunt you down.

We'll see.

The chat window closed. She was gone.

Mav sank back in his chair. She'd be back. He knew it.

What the hell did she want? His gut hardened. She was no doubt a thief, and after something.

His cell phone rang. "Rivera."

"Sir, it's Alex from Security. We had a system breach. He got a few layers in, and we couldn't track him."

"Thanks, Alex. Increase the intrusion detection and enhance the firewalls. Keep me informed."

"Yes, sir."

Mav stared at the angel-wing image. *Who the hell are you?*

3

YOU SHOULDN'T PLAY AROUND ON LADDERS

Remi

Adrenaline pumped through me and left me a little jittery.

I hefted my toolbox and the lightweight aluminum ladder, and headed into the front of the Rivera Tech office building in lower Manhattan.

My brown coveralls were baggy, and I had a tool belt slung around my hips, and a brown ball cap pulled on my head. Across the top of it was stitched *Atlas Electric*.

I headed to the security desk, pasting on a smile.

I'm just a nobody electrician headed to work. Nothing to see here.

"Hi," I called out. "I'm here from Atlas Electric to do a job." I lifted a scrap of paper. "Some maintenance on the 49th floor for Rivera Tech."

The guard frowned, and tapped onto the computer in front of him. "We have you down for tomorrow."

HACKING MR. CEO

"Yeah. I finished a job round the corner, so they sent me here. Someone was supposed to call."

The guy glanced at my toolbox and ladder. "Show me some ID, and let me search your gear."

I rested the ladder against the desk and hefted the toolbox onto the bench. I pulled out my Atlas Electric ID that I'd made myself. I'd burned my finger on the laminator.

Man, Maverick Rivera was paranoid.

Maverick Rivera. I smiled as the guard searched my toolbox. I had my tablet in there, but at a cursory glance, that was nothing that an electrician shouldn't have.

I couldn't believe I'd played hacker footsie with the big man himself. The guy had minions. Hell, his minions probably had minions, and yet, he still monitored his own system. I felt a faint prickle of unease.

I'd analyzed the data from my flyby. I'd tapped my gray-hat contacts. Everyone said hacking more than a few layers into the Rivera Tech couldn't be done. So here I was, going into the dragon's lair. I was going to place my little angel directly into the system.

I hated the terms trojan, or virus, or malware. My sweet little angel was pure beauty.

I'd hacked Atlas Electric—it had been ridiculously easy—and I saw they were sending someone tomorrow to fix an electric issue at Rivera Tech.

That person would still turn up, never knowing that I'd visited today.

"There you go." The guard handed my ID back. "Elevator seven."

With a nod, I grabbed the toolbox and ladder—both

31

of which I'd nabbed from Steve's garage—and headed for the elevator.

I maneuvered my ladder inside and kept my face hidden and looked at the floor. I knew where all the cameras were. If they did get tipped off, they wouldn't get a good look at me.

Rivera only had a small office in the city. He had a big sprawling complex with labs and manufacturing warehouses called Rivera Tech Park, upstate near Syracuse. I would kill to get in there, but it had much tougher security. They had prototypes up there, so they were extra cautious.

But here in the head office, it was easier for a desperate, enterprising hacker trying to save her mother to slip inside.

The elevator slowed, and I hefted the ladder and toolbox.

The place was all open plan. It was dotted with sleek desks, and breakout spaces with colorful couches. At the back were huge touchscreens on the wall and people stood at them touching their fingers against the data and code.

I itched to look at it, but I forced myself to walk to the reception desk.

A young man and woman were seated behind the polished, high desk. The woman looked up at me—she had funky, blue hair.

"Ah, the electrician for the lights that aren't working," the woman said. "Let me show you."

The woman led me back toward the back of the offices.

Now, the layout of the floor changed. There were several doors leading into some conference rooms and offices. As we walked past one office, I glimpsed a computer on the desk.

I stifled a gasp. It was a Rivera Tech Ultra400. It wasn't even on the market yet.

Pure need filled me. I'd sell my kidney for one.

"Here." The receptionist pointed up. "These lights are either off, or they flicker. Benji from Accounting almost had an epileptic fit."

"Got it," I said. "I'll take a look."

I set up my ladder. I'd gotten the schematics of the building. If I was correct, I should be able to find the computer cabling in the ceiling and tap into it.

Humming, I climbed up the ladder and pushed the ceiling panel up. I poked my head in.

Bingo.

I spotted a huge wad of cables of all different colors and grinned. Standing on the top rung, I fished around. I needed the network cable, and I needed not to electrocute myself.

I gripped the blue cable and smiled. *Come to mama.*

Carefully, I climbed back down and rifled through my toolbox. I grabbed my tablet and some pliers, then climbed back up.

Quickly, I spliced the cable and plugged my tablet in.

There. I was in the Rivera Tech network.

I couldn't help but feel it was like cheating. A good hacker liked to storm the castle and get through the defenses with wit and cunning, not sneak in like this. Well, a girl had to do what a girl had to do.

I couldn't afford to stay long, but I wouldn't need to.

Tapping on my screen, I quickly copied my little angel into the system.

"Go, little gal." It would quietly sneak around and give me a way in later.

I glanced at all the other wiring. I had no clue how to fix the lights. If I tried, I'd likely electrocute myself.

Carefully, I disconnected my tablet and stuck it in one of my pockets. Then I taped up the cable.

Adrenaline zinged through me.

"Mav, I put those financial reports on your desk," a voice said.

"Did you have to?" a deep voice replied.

I froze.

Maverick Rivera.

Don't, Remi. Let him pass.

Ooh, but I really wanted to look at the man in person. I climbed halfway down the ladder and my body stilled.

Oh, crap. Photos of the guy did him no justice.

He was standing nearby, in dark suit pants and a crisp, white shirt. He was scowling at a tall, lean guy in a suit.

Rivera was big. A few inches over six feet, with broad, broad shoulders. They stretched his shirt to the extreme. He might be a billionaire, but he looked like he could heft a broadsword and take it to the battlefield.

He had black hair, a little shaggy and in need of a cut, a rugged face, and that gorgeous black stubble on his cheeks and firm jaw.

I whimpered quietly. Yep, I was a sucker for stubble. I had a thing for the bad boys.

"Read the reports, Mav," the man said, sounding determined.

Rivera grunted. He turned and walked away.

I leaned out, trying to keep him in view.

Oh, man, the guy's ass was prime fantasy material.

The ladder shifted beneath me.

Oh, shit.

I tried to right myself, failed and overcorrected, and the ladder started tilting. I sucked in a breath. It all happened so fast.

I fell and hit the floor on my back. The air rushed out of me with an *oof*.

The ladder, thankfully, didn't land on top of me. It hit the floor beside me with a clatter.

A rugged face came into view, dark brows pulled together. Maverick Rivera in full, close-up glory.

"You okay?"

His voice held the edge of a growl.

I sat up. "I think so."

"You have a death wish? You shouldn't play around on ladders."

My anger spiked. *Thank you, Captain Obvious.* "Yes, I totally woke up today and thought, I know, let's fall off a ladder."

His scowl deepened.

I leaped to my feet, then made a shooing motion. "Run along, I need to finish my work."

His eyebrows went up. Ah, I bet the grumpy billionaire was used to bowing and scraping, not smartasses.

"What did you say?" he said.

"Oh, is this where you use the old 'do you know who I am?' line. Because I hope you aren't that clichéd."

"I think you must've hit your head." With a disgruntled noise, he stomped off.

He might be a big lump of grumpiness, but the man's ass was still bitable.

Right. *Time to go.*

I'd tell blue-hair lady at reception that I needed to order some parts, and that someone would be back tomorrow.

Then I'd get home and wait for my angel to give me a way in.

Mav

Mav let himself into his penthouse.

"Lights."

The lights clicked on. It'd been a long day, with an afternoon of endless meetings. He shrugged out of his jacket and tossed it over a chair.

He had some leftover empanadas to eat. His mom had made a huge batch for him last time she'd visited.

Then he wanted to check if his hacker had been back.

He hadn't received an alert, so, if she had revisited, she hadn't set off any alarms.

He stepped into the kitchen, and set his laptop on the huge island. He grabbed a beer from the fridge and popped the top. It was a microbrew he liked. He'd found the brewery on the trip upstate with Zane and Liam one long weekend.

He sipped the beer and leaned against the island. There'd be no more guys' trips away, now. Zane and Liam had snagged women they wanted to keep. They'd be having romantic weekends away.

Mav sighed.

It wouldn't be the same, but he'd still spend time with them, and with Monroe and Aspen.

His laptop chimed with a call. He saw his mother's name and smiled.

He touched the screen. "Hey, Mom."

"There's my boy."

He had the perfect view of one of his mother's dark eyebrows.

Mav rolled his eyes. No matter how many times he showed her the tablet camera and how to get it right, the lesson never stuck.

"Wait, wait," Maria Rivera said. "There."

Her smiling face came into view.

She was going gray and didn't care. She'd told him, *I raised four children, Maverick, I've earned those grays.*

His parents still lived in the same apartment Maverick had grown up in in the Bronx. He'd tried to buy them something else, but they refused. He'd paid off their mortgage and updated the place for them, at least.

"You don't look like you're eating enough." Her gaze narrowed on the beer. "You can't drink beer for dinner."

"Mom, I just walked in the door. I'm about to heat up some of your empanadas."

She looked slightly mollified. Then she licked her

lips. "So, I saw your photo in the paper. You were at some party."

Mav grunted. He went to far too many parties for his own liking.

"You were with a blonde. She was very beautiful. I think her name was Alyssa. They said you're dating."

His hand curled around the bottle. "I told you not to read that crap, Mom. They make shit up."

"Maverick, that mouth."

He pressed a hand to the back of his neck. "I met that woman at the party. We talked for three minutes. That's it."

His mother's shoulders slumped. "So you aren't dating?"

"No, Mom. I don't date."

Her face got a look. Shit, he hated that look.

"Your brothers and sister are married. I have two grandbabies."

"So you should be happy."

"I want *you* to be happy, Maverick."

"Mom, I am happy." He waved an arm at the sleek kitchen.

His mother made a harrumphing sound. "All alone in that giant place. That's not happy."

"I love my work and I have good friends. I'm happy."

"Your friends have women now."

"Yes," he conceded through gritted teeth.

"You need a good woman. One who makes you laugh, and who doesn't let you get your own way all the time."

"Mom—"

"It's all *that* woman's fault," his mother spat.

God, Mav didn't want to talk about Hannah. "No, I—"

"She was all gloss, but rotten inside. None of us saw it."

"It was a long time ago." He knew his mother needed to run out of steam, get it out of her system again, so it didn't really matter what he said.

"Yes, so you should stop letting what she did still control your life."

He stayed silent. He just needed to wait until his mother was done.

She stared at him. Sighed.

His father walked past behind his mother. "Hi, Mav."

"Hi, Dad."

Hector Rivera was as tall as Mav, but had a lean, wiry body. He grabbed a beer from the fridge and disappeared.

"How are Linc and Nora?" Mav asked.

Asking about the grandkids was a surefire way to distract his mom.

"I know what you're doing." She shot him a resigned look, then she smiled. "They're great. Nora is crawling now, and Lincoln drew me a new picture." She pointed a finger at the painting stuck to the fridge.

"Ah, it's very colorful," Mav said.

"It's a bus," his mom said proudly.

It looked vaguely like a yellow-and-green hurricane to him. "Right. I'd better get going, Mom."

"All right, Maverick. Come to dinner soon." A pause. "Bring a girl, if you like."

Not happening. "*Te quiero*, Mom."

"*Te quiero, hijo mio.*"

Mav ended the call. Just then, his computer pinged.

His pulse spiked. It was a security alert.

He tapped on the keyboard and brought up his monitoring program.

Hmm, a hacker was skimming again. He trailed the hacker. They weren't delving deep, but all his instincts told him it was the same hacker as last night. His guess was that she was a gray hat. Flexing her skills for the thrill of the challenge.

He opened the chat window and took a chance.

You're back.

I'm back.

It was *her*.

I warned you. I'm going to track you down.

You wish. You might be the mighty Maverick Rivera, but you aren't God.

God, another smartass. He'd already had a tiny, feisty electrician snip at him today.

I'm the God of my system.

He set his tracker to work, but he suspected she was too slippery for him to trace. He'd have to work a lot harder to pin this hacker down.

So you aren't busy, out buying a yacht or test-driving a new sports car?

Mav shook his head and typed.

No.

You're not out buying a new tuxedo, or jewels for your supermodel girlfriend?

I don't have a girlfriend.

Shame, might sweeten your disposition.

He frowned. What did she mean by that?
Do you have a boyfriend?

You don't know for certain that I'm a girl. And maybe I like girls.

She was female.
You're avoiding the question.

No, I don't have a boyfriend.

Why are you back poking at my system, Ms. Hacker? Just for the thrill?

No.

He frowned.

Have you ever made a bad mistake, Rivera?

He thought of Hannah.
Yes.

*Well, I made one, but for the right reasons, of course.
I'm totally sighing dramatically over here.*

Mav's lips twitched.
You can recover from bad mistakes.

I hope so. I just...

The cursor blinked.
What?

Regret that some people will get hurt.

Mav felt a shiver down his spine.
Why are you here?

There was no response, and he realized that she was gone.

4

GUILT WAS A SUCKY EMOTION

Remi

"Remi, are you listening?"

I blinked and looked at Killian. I was pretty sure my boss wasn't used to being ignored.

"Are all those jobs I sent you okay?" he asked.

I nodded and looked at the list again. They were all straightforward testing of systems. One client had been targeted with some brute force attacks, and another with a DDoS attack—Distributed Denial of Service. I'd map their vulnerabilities and report back to Killian.

Nothing I couldn't handle.

"Are you all right?"

I glanced at Killian's hawkish face. I needed to pull myself together. "Yes. Sorry. I...fell off a ladder today." *Oh, and I have to hack a billionaire tech CEO.*

I totally wasn't sharing that with Killian.

My boss' dark eyes said he didn't believe me.

"All right, well, I'll wait to get your report." He

paused. "Remi, I take care of my employees. If you need anything, you can come to me."

I needed almost one million dollars. Killian couldn't help Mama, but I could.

"Thanks, Killian."

I closed the call and a notification popped up. A message from my hacker buddy, Wesley.

Hey, Remi. Haven't talked for a while. How about we grab a coffee and I can show you my latest botnet tracker?

Ugh. Eventually, I was going to have to have a frank discussion with Wesley. I closed the message and glanced at the screen with my angel data displayed. She was floating through the Rivera Tech system. She'd find a way in for me.

A glance at my watch made me wince. *Crap.* I was late for dinner.

I hustled over to Mama Alma's and was met with chaos. Everyone was at the kitchen table. Adults were scooping food onto plates, the boys were yelling about some video game they were playing, and Kaylee was giggling.

"You're late, child," Mama said.

"Sorry." I slipped into my chair. "I got caught up with some work."

Mama met my gaze. "You're going to work yourself into the ground."

I heard the warning in her voice.

"I won't." It was a lie. I'd do anything for Mama. I'd work my fingers to the bone for years if I had to.

But Mama didn't have years.

My stomach was a giant knot and all I could do was pick at my casserole.

My thoughts turned to Maverick Rivera. *Wow.* The guy was gorgeous, grumpy, and smart. It was a hell of a combination, and it sure appealed to me. Thoughts of those dark-brown eyes and the stubble on his jaw made me suppress a shiver. I was pretty sure he could be an asshole. I sighed. I kind of even liked that. I liked our little cat-and-mouse game.

But once he knew what I was up to, then he'd hate my guts.

Guilt was a sucky emotion. I felt like I was coated in filth.

"Earth to Remi," Steve said.

I jerked my head up and found everyone looking at me. "Sorry."

"You've barely touched your food," Mama said.

"I know. I'm not hungry. I have a lot on my mind." I rose and took my plate to the sink. "I've got some more work I need to finish..."

I felt a tug on my jeans and found Kaylee in front of me. The little girl hugged me and my throat closed.

I dropped to my knees and hugged her back. "Love you, KayKay."

She touched my nails. "Uh-oh."

A couple were chipped. Probably thanks to my stint as an undercover electrician.

I smiled. "I might paint them tonight. What color should I do?"

The little girl cocked her head and grinned. "Red, with sparkles."

"Deal."

"Me too?" She held out a hand, a hopeful look on her face.

"No," Steve said from the table.

Kaylee pouted. I tweaked her nose. "When you're bigger, Princess."

I walked past the others, and ruffled Jamal's and Charlie's hair. "Be good."

"Never," Charlie growled like a pirate.

Beside him, Naomi rolled her eyes.

I dropped a kiss to Mama's cheek.

She grabbed my hand. "None of us are alone, Remi. We're a family."

A family she'd made. Love filled me.

I couldn't let our family be broken. I'd had enough broken families to last me a lifetime.

I headed through the smaller side door into the auto shop. Everything was dark and quiet. Back in my loft, I made a beeline straight for my computer.

Nothing yet from my angel. I tapped my fingers on the desk. I was terrible at waiting.

I pulled out my nail kit and removed my old nail polish. I started work on blood red, with sparkle flecks in it. Mama had given me my first manicure a week after I'd come to her.

"You choose what color, Remi," she'd said. "They're your nails, it's your choice."

No one had ever given me a choice before.

Over the years, I'd become obsessed with pretty polishes. No matter what life threw at me, my nails were always colorful.

As I waited for the polish to dry, I awkwardly tapped in a search on Maverick.

I really, really didn't want to steal from him. Corporate espionage left me feeling sick.

But a few days had already passed and my deadline was looming. My stomach heaved.

The guy was a billionaire, right? He'd bounce back if I stole some fancy design or program for my mystery employer.

The Calix Project. Again, I wondered what it was.

Some recent articles on Rivera popped up. There was a picture of him in a tuxedo at some fancy fundraiser. My entire body pulsed. The guy looked like he didn't want to be at the shindig. He was scowling, but boy, oh boy, the tuxedo fit him so well.

I indulged a moment, imagining taking the suit off him.

Mmm.

Clearly it had been far too long since I'd had sex. The last guy I'd dated had been some banker from the city. We'd dated, slept together a few times, and then he'd ghosted me. *Asshole.*

Before him was a tattooed mechanic with a sexy motorcycle. We'd had fun, until I'd dropped in unannounced, and found him having sex with some short-skirted biker babe on the sexy bike.

My track record with men was not great.

The next article on Rivera was from some trashy gossip site. It was a grainy picture of him in a fancy bar. A flashy blonde in a tight dress was leaning into him. It looked like the picture had been taken from someone's phone.

Man, it must suck to have people taking pictures of you all the time.

I studied the stacked blonde. She was the complete opposite of me.

The next picture was of him with Zane Roth and Liam Kensington. The billionaire bachelors.

Roth was your typical tall, dark, handsome, and rich. Liam Kensington looked like a prince—tall, golden, handsome, and rich.

There were two women in the shot, as well. It was from a party just this week. It appeared that the billionaire bachelors of New York were dropping like flies.

Zane was living with a locksmith store owner named Monroe O'Connor. Liam had recently been targeted by some crazy blackmail plot involving a gangster treasure and white-collar criminals. He'd fallen in love with a private investigator, Aspen Chandler. Their story was still all over the news.

The next shot was Maverick with his family.

I froze. There was a group of them, all dark-haired and brown-skinned. He had his arm around a curvy, comfortably plump, older woman. His mother. Behind them, his father was smiling, and so was Maverick.

Ha, so the man could actually smile. I stared at him. It was a hell of a smile.

I wondered what it felt like when he smiled at you like that.

I shook my head.

He wouldn't be smiling at me. *Ever*.

It was clear that he loved his family. My gut curdled. Hell, maybe he was a decent guy.

And I had to hack his system and steal the Calix Project.

I squeezed my eyes shut. A headache was building. My computer chimed and I leaned forward. Then I gasped.

My little angel had given me a way in. It was still undetected.

I pulled in some deep breaths, and sent another silent apology to Maverick Rivera.

Okay, time to have a poke around at Rivera Tech.

Mav

Mav sat at the head of the conference table, his hands steepled in front of him, listening to the joint venture partner drone on.

He hated late-evening meetings. Outside, through the windows, the lights of Manhattan gleamed and twinkled.

Mav felt his CFO glaring at him and flicked a glance at Richard on his left. The man rolled his eyes wildly.

Mav grunted. *Yeah, yeah, I'm listening.*

He refused to just hand over the business side of Rivera Tech to a CEO. He'd prefer it, because then he could spend all his hours in his lab, but it seemed too many people lost their companies after trusting the wrong people.

Rivera Tech was *his*. He'd keep his fingers in every inch of it, even if it bored him to tears.

"We'll be looking to spread manufacturing of the new tablets over several locations—" the man presenting continued, pointing to a large screen on the wall filled with graphs and charts.

Mav had already been over the production plan and budget. Consumers were clamoring for the new Riv 5+ phone.

He just wanted his team to get on with it.

His phone—a prototype 6+—vibrated in his pocket. He pulled it out and glanced at it.

His chest locked.

He had an urgent message from Rollo.

NEED YOU! NOW!

Mav rose. The presenter stumbled to a halt, and Richard gave him a narrow stare.

"I'm sorry. Something important has come up. Richard will stay here as my proxy."

Maverick didn't wait for questions. He strode out of the conference room, buttoning up his suit jacket as he went.

He marched down the hall and burst into an office.

It was dark. Only the blue glow from the screens illuminated the man sitting in front of them. Rollo, munching on chips, and radiated nervous tension.

"Rollo?"

The man turned his head and blinked.

Rollo's brown hair had left windswept far behind, and could only be classed as wild and crazy. He had a round face with a high forehead, and large, brown eyes.

"Hey, Mav-man."

"What have you got?" Mav pressed a hand to the back of Rollo's chair and leaned in.

"We have an intruder."

"What?"

"We've got a trojan cruising the system. It's clever. It doesn't stop, and it isn't leaving much of a trail."

Mav's gut tightened. "Has anyone hacked in?"

"Nope."

Fuck. "Did it come in via an email or something an employee accessed?"

"Nope."

Rollo, a man of few words. "So someone connected to the system internally to upload it, or had an employee do it."

Rollo munched on another chip with a crunch. "Yep."

"Fuck." Mav pressed a hand to his hip. "Can you flush it out?"

"Trying to catch it is the problem."

There was a soft ping from Rollo's computer and Mav's phone.

"Someone's connecting to the trojan to make their way in!" Rollo straightened. "Fuckers."

Mav's gut told him exactly who it was.

Her.

"I'll take care of this."

"What?" Rollo straightened.

"Leave this to me."

Mav strode out, and down the corridor. At the end, he stormed into his office. When he'd outfitted the River

Tech offices, the designer had wanted to fill his office with stuff. Useless stuff, like vases and statues. He'd vetoed that, so his office had a dark-wood floor, and sleek, austere lines. He had a large, modern desk, and a great view of the city. Minimalist to the extreme.

Mav dropped behind his computer and the screens flared. He tapped, then swiped the touchscreen.

There.

He saw his visitor zooming through his system.

"Where are you going, Little Ms. Hacker?"

His shoulders tensed. He'd been sure she was just a thrill seeker. Now, he wasn't so sure.

She looked like she had no plan. He tapped his fingers on the desk and studied how her trojan worked.

It flitted all over the place. Interesting. He definitely wanted to take a closer look at it.

Mav saw her pause. For a second, he thought she was gone.

Then he saw where she was headed, and cursed.

She was going into the confidential, top-secret files. Where designs of future projects were stored.

There were many classified projects in there. Some were government, including one with the DOJ, and another with the military.

He couldn't let her in. He tapped and activated his own program that he affectionately called the dragon.

It threw up a protective wall around the files.

"You're *not* getting through that," he muttered.

She paused again.

Mav opened a chat window.

I see you.

Busted.

Couldn't hack your way in, so you snuck in the old-fashioned way.

A girl's gotta do what a girl's got to do.

He felt a slow simmer of anger.
What are you after?

I can't tell you.

You're not just a gray hat.
There was a pause.

No. Sorry.

Sorry? He frowned and remembered Hannah had been sorry too, after he'd discovered her real reason for fucking him.
You can't have any schematics. You're just another fucking thief.

You don't understand!!!

Sick of typing, Mav took a risk and opened an audio channel.

"I'm very used to frauds, thieves, and scam artists. You find a little success, and they all come out of the woodwork. They want something, need something, and they lie to get it. They don't want to work their asses off, just expect to take what's mine."

Chest heaving, he waited.

The silence stretched on and he figured she wasn't going to respond.

"I am sorry, Rivera."

He straightened. A smoky, female voice. Brooklyn accent. His pulse leaped.

"You're sorry I caught you," he said.

"You haven't caught me yet." There was a heavy dose of sass in her voice.

"I will hunt you down. You are not taking anything of mine. I have the time, resources, and skills to hunt you to the ends of the earth."

He heard her breathing come across the line.

"Man, someone was really mean to you when you were little. Is that it? Look, you wouldn't understand, but I'm out of options—" Her voice hitched.

Mav leaned back in his chair.

"I don't have any good choices," she continued. "Only a really bad one." She sighed. "I hate being backed into a corner."

Mav did too.

"I hate that I have to hack your system and take something of yours. But if I don't do this..."

God, just another sob story. He ground his teeth together. He should just track her down and have her arrested.

His fingers curled.

"Tell me," he said. "Tell me who's forcing you to do this?"

5

TRAITOR

Remi

Maverick's deep voice echoed in my ears.

God, I wanted to share. To unload this burden. I pulled in a shaky breath. *No.* He'd be the one to suffer from this.

"Like I said, I'm sorry. I wish things could've been different. But the life of someone I love dearly is at stake."

"You said you didn't have a boyfriend."

"I don't. You'll shake this off. My...the person I love won't, unless I do this. I'm so sorry. I have to go." I lifted a hand.

"No, *don't.*"

His voice stopped me. Nothing good would come from interacting with him, but I couldn't make myself end the call.

"You got into my system," he said. "Tell me how. I need to work on my security."

"Actually, big guy, I had to sneak into your office to plant my angel."

He grunted.

"But now I'm in here, I see a few places where you could beef things up."

"Oh, really?" he drawled.

"Hey, don't get defensive. You asked, and nobody's perfect."

He made a sound—part snort, part rusty laugh. I felt it in my belly. This man was dangerous.

I rattled off a few suggestions where his system had weak points.

"You know your stuff," he said grudgingly.

"I do." *Crap.* I needed to be careful that I didn't give too much away. "Anyway, a few tweaks and your system will be rock solid. I mean, it's good now..."

"Thanks," he said dryly.

I closed my eyes. Right, me telling a tech billionaire that his system was good.

There was a blip on my screen. My angel had gone deeper.

It had gotten a hit on the Calix file.

I heard a muted alarm and realized it was coming through Maverick's audio.

Oh, shit.

"Fuck. You're after the Calix Project."

"Rivera—"

"I'm a fucking idiot."

His raw anger came across loud and clear, and my mouth went dry. "Rivera—"

"Once again, I let myself get fooled. I thought first

you were just a gray hat, then some innocent being forced to do this."

"I am!"

"Bullshit. You're not just a thief out for a big paycheck, you're a traitor."

"What?" I breathed.

"A traitor to your country."

I shook my head. "No—"

"The Calix Project is a government military project. To do with the entire system security of our military."

I sucked in a breath. My chest hurt. "*No.*"

"You had to know, or you're an idiot."

"*Hey.*" I felt my own temper stir.

"Do you even know who you're working for?" He made an angry sound. "They could be a foreign enemy, terrorists—"

My stomach turned. I felt nausea crawl through my body.

No. No. No.

I hadn't let myself think. I pressed a hand to my churning belly. My hand shook.

"You're *not* getting that project," Maverick growled. "And I will find you, then I'm going to send you to jail."

He cut the audio.

I slammed my laptop closed. My stomach twisted, and I ran to the bathroom and dropped to my knees by the toilet. I brought up what little dinner I'd eaten.

Flushing, and feeling miserable, I rinsed my mouth and staggered to my bed.

I sat in the rumpled covers, knees to my chest.

Shit. What did I do now? If I continued this hack and

handed over the Calix Project, I could be abetting enemies of my country. I could endanger soldiers' lives.

If I didn't, I was condemning Mama to die.

Tears welled and rolled down my cheeks. On top of all of that, Maverick Rivera had vowed to hunt me down and have me arrested.

I hadn't felt this alone since before I'd come to Mama's foster home.

I couldn't share with my family.

I couldn't share with anybody.

I had no idea what the hell I was going to do.

Mav

Early the next morning, Maverick strode into his trainer's gym.

Simeon was a former Israeli soldier. He liked to beat Mav, Zane, and Liam's asses on a regular basis.

Growing up, Mav had been pretty decent with his fists, and Simeon had honed that.

Mav's eyes were gritty. He'd slept badly. He'd spent half the night working to find his hacker. He'd spent the other half twisting and turning in his bed, gnawing on his anger.

Fucking hacker.

Another selfish woman thinking of no one but herself. Like Hannah. His hacker said it was for a loved one. He snorted. Excuses. The same as Hannah had used.

He got on the treadmill to warm up. He ran hard and fast until he was sweating.

Then he walked over to the large climbing wall.

A good, hard climb was what he needed.

He pulled on a set of climbing shoes, yanked his shirt off, and clipped a chalk bag to his belt. He pressed his hands to the wall. No harness. He was up for a free solo climb.

He picked the hardest route. He moved upward and leaped to grab a handhold.

Grunting, he pulled himself up the wall.

Soon, his muscles burned. Good. He wanted the pain. It pushed out everything else. He dusted some chalk on his hands.

He shouldn't be this angry. He didn't even know his mystery hacker.

He wasn't focused, and missed the next handhold. His body slid partway down the wall, and he muttered a string of curses. He managed to catch himself.

"What the *hell* are you doing, Mav? You fall, you'll break your neck."

He glanced down. Zane, Liam, and Simeon were watching. Zane and Liam were both frowning. Simeon had his arms crossed over his chest.

Mav took a deep breath, and finished the last few meters of the climb.

He took his time climbing down.

"What's going on?" Liam asked.

Mav stripped off the chalk bag. "Nothing."

Zane stabbed a finger at the wall. "That was *not* nothing."

"I'm just working out some things."

"So do it with a harness on," Zane said.

Simeon's eagle-eyed gaze was on him. "Woman trouble."

Shit. Mav kept his face blank.

Zane shook his head. "Mav doesn't let women close enough to cause him trouble."

Liam nodded. "They get a few hours of his time in a swanky hotel room, that's it."

Mav grunted, and grabbed his water bottle. He stayed silent.

Zane's eyebrows winged up. "Shit, it is a woman."

Mav scowled. "No."

"Who is she?" Liam asked.

"Are we going to work out or what?" Mav demanded.

"Avoidance," Liam said. "Definitely woman trouble."

Mav sighed. "No, I have a hacker problem."

Simeon watched him intently. "And the hacker is a woman?"

They weren't going to let it go until he gave them *something*. "Yes."

"Ah," Liam said.

Zane smiled. "Really?"

"She's after the Calix Project."

"Oh, shit," Zane said.

"Big military project," Liam told Simeon. "National security."

Mav ran a hand through his sweat-damp hair. "I've been tracking her movements, and talking with her for a few days."

"You liked her," Liam said.

Mav heard understanding in Liam's voice. He'd been in a similar spot with Aspen. At first, he thought she'd been blackmailing him.

Mav shook his head. "This hacker is just another user."

"What are you going to do?" Zane asked.

"Protect my project, then track her ass down and hand her over to the police. I spent half the night enhancing my tracker program. I *will* find her."

"Okay. If you need any help, we're here," Zane said.

Liam nodded.

Mav's chest tightened. "Thanks, guys. Now, can we please spar?"

They paired off. Mav faced Simeon on the mats. The man might be several pounds lighter, and several decades older, but it paid to never underestimate Simeon.

An hour later, Mav was sweating and breathing hard.

He dodged Simeon's kick, but a second later, took a punch to the side.

He grunted.

"Your head's not in the game," Simeon said.

Mav stomped to his water and chugged. His phone chimed, and he snatched it up and thumbed the screen.

He hissed. He stared at the map and the glowing, red dot on it.

His tracker had worked.

He'd found her.

Sunset Park in Brooklyn.

He smiled.

"Uh-oh, he's smiling," Liam said.

Mav glanced at his friends. "I need to go."

"Where?" Zane demanded.

"Out."

"*Mav.*" Zane scowled.

"It's fine. I'm not going to do anything crazy."

Zane shook his head, and Liam just arched a brow.

Mav quickly showered, and changed back into the jeans and tan suede jacket he'd worn to the gym, ignoring his suit he'd planned to wear to the office. He headed out to his car.

The sleek, red Rivera roadster wasn't exactly low profile. Rivera Tech had started producing electric cars two years ago. The roadster wasn't available yet, but he knew it would be a success. It was a sweet ride.

Mav liked cars and had a small collection—an Aston Martin DB11, a Mercedes CLK GTR AMG Roadster, and Ferrari 812 Superfast, among others.

He headed out of Manhattan, calling his assistant on the way to get her to cancel his morning meetings. The long-suffering Bridget was used to it, but would make him pay. He headed over the Brooklyn Bridge. When he reached Sunset Park, he avoided the street where his hacker was located. The dot hadn't moved. He parked a block away, and headed in that direction on foot.

Slipping his hands in his pockets, he strode down the street. There were rows of older houses, and some industrial buildings at the end of the street. He paused on the other side of the street and pulled out his phone, pretending to look at it.

He discreetly looked across the street and several houses down. The large doors were open at an auto shop.

Then he heard children's laughter. He glanced at the house next door.

A petite, curvy woman was playing with some kids on the steps.

The woman had dark-brown, shoulder-length hair, and held a blonde little girl on her hip. Two boys were play-fighting, with what looked like plastic lightsabers.

The woman turned and smiled.

Mav stilled.

That wide smile lit up a face with a pointed chin, cute nose, and dark brows. Fitted jeans displayed generous curves for such a tiny woman.

"Charlie, you hit me with that, boyo, and I'll make you pay."

Everything in Mav flared to life.

It was *her*.

It was her voice. As he watched, he realized that he knew her.

The smartass electrician who'd fallen off the ladder in the office. That's how she'd gotten the trojan into his system.

"Remi! Remi!" the little girl cried.

"I've got you, KayKay." The woman touched the girl's nose, then set her down. "I smell cookies inside. They should be ready soon."

Mav scowled. She didn't look like a hardened hacker out to make a quick buck.

Don't get fooled for a second time, Rivera.

The front door opened, and an older, African-American woman came out. "Cookies are ready."

The kids cheered.

"Then boys, you need to get to school," the woman continued.

The boys groaned, but raced inside with the little girl.

His hacker, Remi, hugged the older woman and murmured something that he couldn't make out.

"Remi, I'm fine. Quit hovering."

"I love you, Mama, so I'm going to hover."

The older woman swatted Remi's curvy butt. "Get in there and have some cookies before they're gone."

"I will—"

The older woman gasped and swayed.

Remi grabbed her "Mama!"

"I'm fine."

"You're *not*."

"Just a little lightheaded, child." The woman cupped Remi's cheek. "I don't want you to worry."

"You're sick. I can't stop worrying. I'll help you inside."

"No." The older woman straightened. "I'm going in under my own steam."

Mav saw Remi's face twist. "I'll be in shortly."

The older woman disappeared inside and Remi dropped heavily onto the top step. Her face was clouded with sadness.

Mav moved closer, drawn to her, although he wasn't sure why.

What was it about this woman?

Suddenly, her head jerked up and their gazes collided.

Her eyes went wide and she leaped up.

A second later, she pushed through the metal gate, then sprinted down the sidewalk.

Away from him.

Fuck.

Mav powered after her and sprinted across the road.

She was small, but fast. She disappeared around the corner.

Dammit. Mav pushed harder. He took the corner and saw her ahead.

There was a large concrete parking area, enclosed by a chain-link fence and topped with barbed wire.

He saw her drop and wriggle through a small hole at the base of the fence.

He had a perfect view of her curvy ass, cupped by denim.

He stumbled to a halt. There was no way he'd fit through that damn hole.

She rose and dusted her hands off. She looked at him through the fence and he saw her eyes were a golden brown, with darker striations in them.

She was breathing fast, and now he noted her breasts pushing against her shirt.

Goddammit, Rivera.

"Hello, angel," he murmured. "I told you I'd find you."

6

IT GETS WORSE

Remi

Air sawed in and out of my lungs. Maverick Rivera was standing *right* in front of me. Only the thin metal mesh of the fence separated us.

I swallowed. "Please don't hurt my family."

His dark gaze focused on me. He didn't say anything. For a second, he reminded me of my picture of the warrior angel.

I stepped up to the fence and gripped it. "If you do..."

"I'm not going to hurt your family."

The deep growl of his voice shivered through me, and mixed with a surge of relief.

My breath shuddered out of me. "I am sorry. I didn't know what the Calix Project was. I guess I thought it was a design for a new phone, or something."

He continued to stare at me.

"That doesn't make it right," I continued in a rush.

"And I don't know who the people who approached me are. It was stupid, and dangerous."

He put his hand on the fence, an inch from mine.

This close, I felt the heat pumping off his big body.

"I won't hack your system," I said.

"Tell me everything that's going on," he demanded.

He said it like he was used to issuing demands and having them followed.

I shook my head.

"Remi."

I sucked in a sharp breath. He knew my name. I nibbled my bottom lip, my belly churning. I saw his gaze drop to my mouth.

Oh. *Shit.*

My gaze flicked up and I swore I saw desire on his face.

God. I couldn't deal with this. I was attracted to him. Hell, any woman with a pulse would be. And it appeared he felt the same.

Right, because I was a tall, lanky model/actress/socialite. I swallowed a snort. The guy wanted me arrested, not naked.

I was either imagining things, or Maverick Rivera didn't mind sampling new flavors. The man was notorious for having no long-term relationships. Well, I wouldn't be anyone's flavor of the week.

"Look, just forget I ever existed. Go back to your fancy Manhattan pad, and our paths will *never* cross again."

"I want to know who contacted you, and how. I want to find the asshole."

I shook my head. "There is no way to find him. Look, I have to go."

I really needed to get away from him.

His hand moved, his fingers touching mine. Just the smallest touch of our fingers through the mesh.

I gasped. I felt that sensation sear through me. I saw the answering echo in his eyes.

"I'm not going to hurt you, Remi."

"I seem to remember the threat of police and jail." I dragged in a ragged breath. "Actually, I'm glad you stopped me from making an even bigger mistake."

I started to turn away.

"Don't go." His fingers tightened on mine.

I had to go. There was no way a scrappy hacker and a tech billionaire belonged in the same room, let alone breathing the same air.

God. I drank him in. I wished we did though.

Impulsively, I leaned in. He did too.

I pressed my lips to his through the mesh, the wire cold on my skin.

I barely got the faintest taste of him.

Then I turned and ran.

"Remi! *Goddammit.*"

I sprinted onto the next street, and kept running until I was out of breath. Then I slowed to a walk.

Overhead, the clouds churned. There was a storm coming. A cold wind picked up, blowing down the street and I pulled my coat around me.

God, I just kissed Maverick Rivera.

Oh, well. A fun story to tell my future grandkids. I hunched deeper into my coat. My life was still a mess. I'd almost committed treason, and I had no way to pay for Mama's surgery.

My phone vibrated. I had an email. I opened my email app.

Any progress on the job?

I stilled, my insides going cold. The sender was a gibberish string of numbers and letters on a Gmail address.

Who is this? I replied.

Your new employer. You can call me The Shadow.

Oh God. The Shadow.

I tapped in a reply.

No. I'm not taking the job after all.

A second later, a response came back.

You agreed to the terms, Rogue Angel. You can't back out now.

Anger spurted through me. He was trying to intimidate me.

I can, and I have.

Then I'll just have to convince you that completing the job is in your best interests.

There was a photo attached to the message.

I opened it and tasted bile in my throat. *No.*

It was a picture of Charlie, Jamal, and Naomi, with backpacks slung on their shoulders, entering their school.

Four days to the deadline.

The world collapsed in on me. I'd tried to help Mama, but all I'd done was put everyone in danger.

My knees felt like Jell-O, and I wanted to collapse. I bit my lip so hard that I tasted blood.

I turned to head home, my feet leaden. My stomach was so churned up I thought I'd be sick.

What did I do now?

I no longer had bad choices, I had monumentally horrible ones.

Be a traitor, or put my family in the firing line of some shadowy bad guy.

Tears welled, and one slid down my cheek. I swiped it away angrily. Crying wouldn't help. I'd learned that years ago.

My cell phone rang. There was no number on the display, and my gut clenched. Was it The Shadow?

Rage welled and I stabbed the screen. "If you hurt my family, asshole, I will find a way to make you pay, I swear it!"

There was a pause.

"I told you that I wouldn't hurt your family."

The air rushed out of me. Maverick's deep voice.

"Uh, I didn't know it was you."

His voice hardened. "Who did you think it was?"

I swallowed.

"Remi?"

"Does that testy growl make people answer you, because it kind of makes me want to hit you?"

"Who threatened your family, Remi?"

I blinked, realization setting in. He had my cell phone number.

Hell, he was a tech guru who owned half the country. He probably knew my full name, my checking account balance, my bra size. I pressed a hand to my head. "He contacted me."

Maverick cursed.

"Yeah, he's not happy that I told him I wasn't doing the job."

"Meet me."

My hand clenched on my phone. "This isn't your mess, Rivera. You shouldn't wade in. Walk away, and live your shiny, rich life."

"No. Besides, I'm already in this."

I huffed out a breath. "Something tells me you take stubborn to a new level."

"So my friends tell me. Meet me, Remi."

I gnawed on my lip. "Okay. Dave and Buster's, Times Square." I hung up before I could change my mind.

God, I hoped I wasn't making another huge mistake.

Mav

Mav hadn't been into Dave and Buster's since he was a kid. He had a few fond memories of trying to beat his older brothers, Carlos and Daniel, at Mortal Kombat.

He still liked gaming. He had a good setup in his movie room at his penthouse.

He wondered if Remi liked gaming.

The memory of that tiny, barely-a-kiss through the fence hit him. It made things worse. Now he wanted to know what she really tasted like. What sounds she'd make as he thoroughly kissed her.

Fuck.

The sound of the terror in her voice on the phone had him worried.

His gut told him the situation was heading south, rapidly.

"Yeah, go, go, go!" a boy's voice yelled across the arcade.

"She's beating you! Hurry."

Mav rounded some games and found a small crowd of kids gathered around a car racing game. The players sat in simulated cars, and the whine of engines echoed through the air.

"I'm going to catch you!" a boy yelled.

"No, you're not," a female voice said.

Remi.

Mav pushed through the crowd and saw her hands clenched on the steering wheel, a wide-eyed teen beside her.

On the screen, Remi's car crossed the finish line.

"Woo-hoo!" She threw her arms up. "See, kid? Old people can game too."

The boy laughed, and dropped a discreet glance at Remi's breasts.

Mav cleared his throat.

Remi glanced at him, and her smile disappeared.

"I've got to go." She climbed out of the car simulator.

"I'd go too," a hovering teenage girl murmured, her gaze locked on Mav.

Mav took Remi's arm and led her to a quieter part of the arcade.

"How about a game, Rivera?" she asked.

He frowned. "We're not here for games."

She raised a brow. "Afraid that I'll beat you?"

"No."

"Come on, then. I'll even pay."

Mav tried to think the last time a woman—not including his mother or sister, Maribel—had bought him anything.

"All right, Ms. Solano. You're on."

She paused. "You know my name."

"Remina Solano." He'd run a quick search on her. A foster child, cybersecurity consultant at Sentinel Security. Yes, he knew some details, but he wanted to know more.

Alarm bells were ringing in his head. The last time he'd wanted to know more about a woman, she'd been a gold digger.

"Here." Remi stopped beside Space Invaders. "Let's play this."

Space Invaders. He hadn't played it in years. "You're on."

She swiped a card, and the screens blinked and music dinged.

The countdown started.

Three. Two. One. "Go!" Remi said.

Mav jerked the gun. He was competitive by nature. He glanced sideways. Clearly, so was Remi. She was leaning into the game, her mouth open a little, her face focused.

His screen flashed.

"Watch out, Rivera, or you're going to lose," she taunted.

"Hell, no," he growled.

She laughed.

In that moment, he forgot all about their troubles. Forgot everything. They were just a man and woman having fun.

Mav threw himself into the game, shooting down spaceships.

"Come on, Rivera. You need to be faster than that—"

"Watch that cockiness, angel."

She grinned. "It's not cocky if I can back it up."

It was good to see the stress and sadness gone from her face for the moment.

The game time ticked down. He was gaining on her. A moment later, words flashed up. *Game Over*.

She turned and pointed. "Beat you, big guy."

"Only by ten points. And I'm only big because you're tiny."

"Don't change the subject. I won." She did a little dance.

Mav tried not to watch the way her hips moved.

"Best of three," he said.

"You're on. I'll even let you pick the next game."

He picked Pac-Man.

"Let's rumble," she said.

They played the next game, trading good-natured barbs.

God, he was having fun with a woman at an arcade. Zane and Liam would lose it, laughing.

Mav won the second game. That's when he learned that Remi pouted when she lost.

"Okay." She grabbed his hand. "I know what we'll play next."

He felt tingles up his arm, and entwined their fingers.

She stilled. He saw her nails were painted a sparkly red. "Lead on and prepare to go down, angel."

Golden-brown eyes met his gaze.

She cleared her throat and broke the connection.

She tried to pull free, but he held tight. Giving up, she led them to an old-fashioned, pinball machine.

"Old school," he said.

"Think you can handle it?" She cocked a hip, sassy as ever.

"Yes. Let's up the ante."

She shot him a wary look.

"A bet," he said. "If you win, what do you want?"

She scanned around. "Hot dog and fries at the restaurant."

He grimaced. "The food here might kill you."

She grinned. "Your billionaire is showing."

"Fine, a hot dog it is."

"And if you win? Which you won't, what do you want?"

He gave her a slow smile. Her gaze locked on his mouth. "A kiss."

"What?" Her gaze flicked up.

"A proper kiss. With tongue."

She wiped her palms on the jeans.

"Afraid?" he asked.

"No. All right, big guy. Bring it."

"Ladies first."

She attacked the pinball machine like a soldier going into battle.

And she was good.

When she finished, her face was flushed. She gave him a curtsy and he was tempted to swat that curvy ass.

Mav took his position at the machine.

He fought hard, but in the end, he lost by a few points.

"Oh yeah, reigning champion." She pointed to herself. "Right here."

"Come on, champion." He took her arm. "I owe you a hot dog."

"Don't forget the fries. And a cola."

Soon they were seated at a table. Mav's chair was too small, but he liked that their knees kept bumping against each other.

She ate like she gamed—all in, with gusto.

She licked ketchup off her fingers, and Mav felt the action in his cock.

"All right, Remi. Time to talk."

He hated seeing the light leak out of her, and the tension return. He wanted to hug her.

What? Hell, he didn't do hugging.

As he wrestled with the very out-of-the-norm feeling, she fiddled with her cup.

"The woman with you at the house, she's your foster mother?" he asked.

Remi nodded and sighed. "Mama Alma. The most amazing, loving, caring woman in the world. She's sick. She has a tumor and has six months to live." Tears welled in Remi's eyes and she sniffed them back. "The only option is experimental surgery. Expensive experimental surgery."

Crap. She'd told him the truth.

"I panicked. I put my name on a black-hat board on the dark web. They contacted me."

"They?"

"I think it's actually a he. Calls himself The Shadow. I've no idea if it is a him, or a her, or a they. He didn't share a real name."

"And he asked for the Calix Project directly?"

She nodded. "He gave me a week. I have four days left. Or three and a bit."

Damn. Mav sat back in his chair.

Remi blew out a breath. "Maverick—"

He felt a jolt. It was the first time she'd used his name, and he liked hearing it.

"He contacted me after I saw you today," she said.

"And?"

"It gets worse," she whispered.

He reached across the table and took her hand. She visibly started, and stared at their entwined fingers.

"Why are you being so nice to me?" she asked.

"Well, I could tell you that I'm a nice guy, but I'm not really. People say I'm mean, grumpy, and antisocial."

She gave him a faint smile. "No, really?"

"Stow the sarcasm, angel."

Her smile faded. "The Shadow said I can't back out." She tapped at the table with one of her colorful nails. "God, Maverick, they emailed me a photo of my foster siblings walking into school."

Oh, crap.

7

NICE TO OFFICIALLY MEET YOU

Remi

E motions churned inside me—despair and worry leading the way.

Oh, and I was holding hands with a billionaire.

I couldn't make myself let go. He was so big, solid.

He made me feel safe.

His dark gaze was on mine. "I'll pay you twice as much to help me catch The Shadow," he said.

I blinked. "Say what?"

"You string him along while working behind the scenes with me to catch him. I'll give you two million dollars, your foster mother can get her surgery, and I'll also put a security guy in front of your home. Don't worry. It'll be someone discreet. No one will know why he's there."

I just stared at Maverick, my throat tight.

"Remi? Angel?" He squeezed my hand.

"Um... No one's ever really swooped in to help me

with things. Usually I hustle, work hard, take care of things myself." I cleared my throat. "Give me a second."

He got a look on his face that I couldn't quite interpret.

"It's going to be all right," he said.

I really, really want to believe that. "Okay, big guy, you have a deal."

He arched a brow. "I have a name."

"Mr. Tech Billionaire CEO?"

He gave me a grumpy look.

"Maverick," I said.

His lips twitched. He shook my hand. "Nice to officially meet you, Remi."

His hand was big and strong like the rest of him. And I imagined it touching other parts of me.

I snatched my hand back, nabbed a fry, and shoved it in my mouth. I had no business imagining any sort of fantasies with this man.

"So, where do we start?" I asked.

"Get in touch with The Shadow. Tell him you'll do the job, but play reluctant."

"That should be easy enough."

"Tomorrow, come to my office." He cocked his head. "Think you can try a reverse hack?"

"Try to hack him?" I pondered. "Maybe. I can embed something in an email."

Maverick smiled and it lit up his rugged face. "I like the way you think."

"Dude, don't do that."

"What?" He looked confused.

"Smile. You're hot enough as it is, and smiling makes it so much—" I waved a hand.

"You think I'm hot?"

"Oh, come on."

He shrugged. "My friend Liam gets voted the best-looking billionaire bachelor. And Zane gets the sexiest."

"*Pfft.* Sure, Liam Kensington is pretty, and Zane has that tall, dark, and handsome thing going on, but some women like their men rugged, muscular, a little rough."

Maverick leaned forward. "Really? Is that what you like?"

Danger. Danger. "Ah, so, back to the task at hand."

He looked amused. "Right. Come to my office tomorrow. I think you know where it is," he said dryly.

I smiled. "I totally rocked my electrician coveralls."

"Can you get there without being noticed?"

"You think The Shadow is watching me?" I fought a shiver.

"Could be."

"Yes, I can get there. I was a champion at sneaking out to arcades as a teen."

"Good. I'll need you to show me the messages you have from this guy, and we'll find a way to track this asshole down."

I fiddled with my soda cup. "This could be dangerous."

"Yes. That's why he needs to be stopped. He'll keep hiring hackers until they get the Calix Project, and then the security of our nation is at risk."

I bit my lip and nodded.

He was looking at my mouth again. Heat spread through me.

Two teens approached, both of them wearing baggy jeans and hoodies.

"Hey, man, are you Maverick Rivera?"

Mav shook his head. "Nope, but I get that a lot. Gets me good tables at restaurants."

The kids' shoulders drooped. "Figured Rivera wouldn't be at Dave and Busters." They shuffled off.

I shook my head. "You aren't the friendliest guy, are you, Maverick?"

"So my friends tell me." He rose. "You have a way home?"

"Yes, it's called the subway. It's an underground train that the unwashed masses use for a couple of bucks a ride."

"Funny. I'll see you tomorrow, Remi."

I nodded. Strangely, I didn't want him to go. "Tomorrow."

I watched him stride off. Okay, I watched his ass as he strode off.

The man was all kinds of fine.

I took the subway home—my mind churning about the situation, and the fact that I was working with a billionaire.

I shook my head. It had been a crazy few days.

Hoofing it down the street, I turned into our street. Speaking of all kinds of fine. A tall guy was carrying a box into the place across the street. His worn jeans and flannel shirt did nothing to hide his muscled bod. He had dark-brown hair with the hint of a curl, and scruff across his jaw.

Old Mrs. Hansen had been trying to rent the upstairs apartment for ages. I crossed over to the auto shop and pulled out my keys.

When I glanced back, the man was looking at me. When he noticed me watching him, he lifted his chin and walked inside.

The hairs on the back of my neck rose.

Oh, God. Something was off. The guy was too watchful.

My stomach clutched. What if he worked for The Shadow? Was he watching us? What if he snatched one of the kids?

Panicking, I raced up the stairs to my loft. I paced, horrible scenarios playing over and over in my head.

I yanked out my phone and hit the button.

I'd saved Maverick's number as *Big Guy.*

"Remi?"

"Maverick." I dragged in a breath. "There's a *guy* here."

"Where?" His voice was sharp.

"I just got home. There's a guy moving in across the street. A big guy. I saw him watching me."

"Don't worry, he's mine."

"What?"

"There's nothing to worry about. He's one of mine. Boone Hendrix. I hired him to watch your family."

The air rushed out of me. "You organized that fast."

"It's easy to do when you have the resources."

"Oh, that's right, you're filthy rich."

"Most people don't tend to forget that."

She didn't, but she noticed the sexy, stubbled jaw, the muscled body, and the grumpy attitude, first.

"Luckily Boone was in the city, available, and he's very good at his job."

"Okay, well, thanks. I'd better get some sleep. I have to report for duty tomorrow."

"I never asked if it would cause trouble with your work."

"No. I make my own hours and work from home."

"Then I'll see you tomorrow, angel."

My stomach flip-flopped at the pet name. "Tomorrow."

I ended the call and set the phone down.

I took a quick shower and slipped into my pajamas. But as soon as I lay in bed, I felt wired.

Okay, that wasn't exactly the truth. I felt turned on.

I thought of Mav. His big hands holding the controls as he played the games. I leaned over and opened the bedside-table drawer, and pulled out my vibrator.

A few minutes later, when I came, I cried out Maverick's name.

Mav

Maverick was as hard as a rock.

Fuck.

He'd dreamed about Remi. He scrunched the pillow under his head. His bedroom was shadowed, the blinds blocking the morning light, and he shoved the sheet down off his hot body. His cock was swollen and throbbing.

He dreamed of Remi's hands on him, her bright nails scratching his skin. That sassy mouth of hers taking his cock.

He groaned and fisted his erection. He pumped.

Then, he imagined that sweet, curvy body against his.

Hey, big guy. He could almost hear her faint laugh. Like she knew a joke that she wasn't sharing.

He stroked harder. "Take me," he growled.

She would. She was petite, but she'd be all energy and enthusiasm. Whether she was sucking him, or taking his cock.

"*Fuck.*" He gave a hard tug and his body locked. Pleasure was like a hard punch and he spilled on his gut with a tortured groan.

He dropped back, panting.

Damn, if the fantasy of her was this hot...

But first, they had to deal with The Shadow.

Once his pulse had leveled off a little, Mav pushed off the bed and headed to shower and dress. He was meeting Liam and Zane for breakfast, then he'd hit the office and clear as much work as he could before Remi arrived.

He looked at himself in the bedroom mirror.

Shit, he was smiling.

His phone vibrated, letting him know he had a text message.

Big guy, I'm wearing a disguise to your office. No one will know it's me.

He tapped in a reply.
Not those ugly coveralls again.

No. Not even you will recognize me.

Angel, I notice you the second you're in the vicinity.

Aw, a compliment. You flirting with me?

Shit. He wasn't a man to play games. He liked to get to the point and keep things simple.
Yes.
He stared at the dots on the screen, waiting for her reply.

Big guy, billionaires don't flirt with Brooklyn hackers.

I don't actually flirt. Ever.

So, I'm special, then?

He was starting to think she might be.
I seem to want to flirt with you.

Rivera, we have a dangerous job ahead of us. You need to focus.

I'm good at multitasking.

Men say that, but they totally aren't.

He shook his head. So much sass.

See you at the office. Don't be late.

She sent him the emoji face with its tongue poking out.

When he walked into Balthazar, a French restaurant near his penthouse, Liam and Zane were already there.

"Good morning." He sat and looked at the waitress. "Coffee. Black."

He picked up the menu and glanced up to see his friends staring at him. "What?"

"Well, yesterday you were tense and broody as hell, and radiating contained rage," Zane said.

Liam sipped the frothy, sweet coffee he loved. "I thought we might have to bail you out of jail, especially when you didn't return my texts last night to check up on you."

"I was busy," Mav said.

"And here you are, looking...relaxed." Zane leaned back in his chair. "Did you find the hacker?"

Mav had no desire to drag his friends into this mess. They'd both just been through bad situations and both had women to protect now. They'd found some happy and he wasn't going to mess that up.

"I made some progress."

The waitress returned, and he ordered Eggs Benedict.

"You didn't even notice our lovely waitress offering you a better view of her neckline," Zane said.

Mav frowned. "What?"

Liam shook his head and smiled.

Mav's phone pinged. He lifted it.

*Hey, our deal better include you buying me lunch.
I need to be fueled to concentrate properly.*

Mav swallowed a snort.

I'll buy you lunch.

Nothing messy. Not with what I'm wearing today.

Now all Mav could think about was what she could be wearing.

See you soon, big guy.

He turned the phone over, looking forward to seeing her.

"Okay, now he's *smiling*." Zane looked incredulous. "What is going on, Mav?"

"Spill it, Rivera," Liam said.

"I'm not smiling." He drank his coffee. "I have...an interesting project that I'm working, that's all."

Neither of his friends looked convinced.

Mav deflected all questions, hurried through his breakfast, and escaped to his office.

Bridget was already at her desk. She was a thirty-two-year-old, icily elegant blonde, with glasses perched on the end of her nose. She had a frosty demeanor he liked. She kept the wolves—aka anyone who annoyed him—at bay, and ran his schedule with frightening precision.

"I lightened your schedule, but you promised to go through the urgent emails." She looked disgruntled.

He held up a hand. "I'm doing it now."

"You keep asking for miracles, Maverick, and I'll need a raise. Or a holiday home in Bora Bora."

Straight to the point, his assistant. "I'm also expecting a woman. Send her in when she arrives."

Bridget cocked her head. "A woman? What's her name?"

"Her name doesn't matter." Mav walked into his office. He shrugged off his jacket and got to work.

Ugh, emails were one of those necessary evils. He plowed through as many as he could, as quickly as possible.

It was highly likely his blunt replies would make someone cry.

Bridget brought him another black coffee, and he grunted his thanks.

He took a look at some prelim plans from the electric-car division. Made some notes. But at the back of his mind, he was thinking about The Shadow.

Who the hell was he? Mav swiveled in his chair, staring out the window, but not really seeing the view.

If this guy wanted the Calix Project, he wasn't good. At best, he was a corporate spy, out to undermine and steal from Rivera Tech.

At worst...

Mav didn't want to think about the worst.

Whoever this fucker was, Mav would find him, and stop the guy.

The intercom on his desk phone chimed.

"Maverick?" Bridget's crisp voice.

"Yes?"

"There's a Ms. Angel here to see you."

Finally. "Send her in."

A moment later the door opened, and Mav's jaw dropped.

She sailed in, wearing a white dress that hugged her curves with loving affection. A white, faux-fur coat hung off her shoulders, and a black belt circled her tiny waist, accenting her hips and breasts.

She wore her hair up, with a few wisps around her face, and flawless makeup, and giant, designer shades, perched on her nose.

She cocked a hip.

"Good morning, Mr. Billionaire. Ready to track down a bad guy?"

8

DRAGON ANGEL

Remi

O kay, I was pretty sure no man had ever looked at me the way Maverick Rivera was looking at me right now.

Fluttery things took flight in my belly. Like I was something delicious, dipped in chocolate sauce.

I liked it. A lot. Too much.

He rose slowly, that dark gaze running down my body.

I swallowed. "You can't look at me like that." I tried to pull off a tension-breaking laugh. "God, put on a tight dress, and men only think of one thing." I strode over and dumped the coat that I'd borrowed off Naomi on the chair, then I hitched myself onto the corner of his big desk and crossed my legs. "We have bad guys to stop, remember?"

His gaze met mine. God, I wanted to run my hand over that stubble-covered jaw.

"I can't remember my name," he said.

Those words sent a shot of heat through me. "Aw, you can be sweet."

"Not usually." He sounded faintly bemused.

I looked past him and my mouth dropped open. "Jeez, that view. I wouldn't get anything done in here."

Maverick moved closer, and looked like he wanted to touch me.

Boy, I wanted him to touch me. And I'd be happy to do some touching of my own.

But I made myself think of Mama, and whoever was The Shadow.

Whatever they had planned, had to be stopped.

My gaze fell to the computer on the desk. It was sleek and sexy. "What is that?"

"My own build."

I slid off the desk, circled it, and dropped into his fancy, executive chair. It was comfy.

The computer was unlocked and I jiggled the mouse.

"It's rude to just help yourself to a man's computer."

I shot him a look. "Rivera, I'm a hacker."

As I looked at the system specs, I whistled. This was one souped-up machine.

Maverick leaned a hip against the desk, watching me. "You like?"

"Oh, I more than like. I'm in love, and plotting how to sneak this little baby out of here."

That got me a flicker of a smile.

I'd sneak him out, too, if I wasn't highly aware that I'd be flavor of the week and then be left with a shattered heart.

I looked at the way his suit pants stretched over his muscular thighs. Hmm, okay, if I did tangle with him, I'd keep my heart locked up. I could have fun. Make a few fun memories for the future.

"Remi?"

I shook my head. "Sorry, thinking." *About taking you for a ride.* "Shall we get to work?"

"Yes. After you get out of my chair."

I bounced a little. "But it's so comfy."

"Mine."

He dragged a second chair around and I pulled my laptop out and set up beside him, transferring to the other chair.

My laptop was covered in sparkly stickers.

"You have a Rivera Tech laptop," he said.

"Of course," I said. "They are a solid brand at a good price point."

That faint smile again. "Shame you desecrated it."

"My niece said it needed to look prettier. And a sticker never hurt anyone."

"Right, how about we find a bad guy?"

"We need a stealthy little trojan to send to him via email. A sneaky little guest that he welcomes in the front door."

"With a tracker embedded."

"Right. I have my angel that I sent into your system."

"Good. I wanted to see your code up close."

"Mr. Rivera, you can't just ask a woman outright to show you her code. I expect dinner and drinks first, at least."

He gave a low chuckle and it skated down my spine.

God, that sexy laugh. "It's fine," I said. "I'll give you a peek."

"And then I can show you my tracker, and we can meld the two together."

"Now you're asking me to be the mother of your child."

Maverick shook his head and I grinned at him.

I hooked into the Rivera Tech system, and we got to work.

Our fingers flew across our keyboards. We traded info and a few quips. I found working with Maverick was fun.

He was grumpy, liked to brood in silence, and needed me to snap him out of it with a joke, or sometimes an elbow to the ribs, but we worked well together.

The man had a sharp, sexy mind.

God, I was a goner. I was mildly turned on, excitement a low-level hum inside me.

"There." I sat back and sipped the coffee that his scary, beautiful assistant had delivered, along with a tray of delicious sandwiches. They were weird, fancy combinations, but mouthwatering. I was trying to stop from eating too many.

"I think we've done it." Maverick nodded. "It's beautiful."

My angel was now a dragon angel, with Maverick's tracker entwined in the code.

"You are a genius, Maverick."

"Right back at you, Remi. And it's Mav. That's what my friends call me."

I turned my head and sucked in a breath. Our faces were inches apart. "Am I your friend, Mav?"

His gaze ran down my face and settled on my lips. "No. I'm not sure I want you to just be my friend."

I leaned closer...

A notification chimed on the laptop, and I jerked.

Damn. I glanced at the screen, and all the nice, buzzy feelings curdled.

"It's The Shadow."

Still on board, Rogue Angel?

I stared at the message for a beat, then typed.

I don't want to be, but yes. I said I'd do it, so I'll do it.

*If your conviction falters, I will take measures
to convince you to deliver what I want.*

I said I'd do it.

"Asshole. He's threatening me."

"Yes, he is," Mav said darkly.

There were no more messages.

I dragged in a breath. "Let's see if we can track this asshole down."

"Send him a message. An update."

I nodded. "I could send them something from the Rivera Tech system. Something non-vital, but proves that I'm getting close."

He nodded. "And hide our dragon angel in it. Brilliant." He cupped my jaw. 'I'll get you a file.'

Where his fingers touched me, my skin felt like it was on fire.

I cleared my throat. "Okay, let's do it."

I could do this. I could work with dark, hot Maverick Rivera and not totally lose all my senses.

Okay, I was *pretty* sure I could.

Mav

Mav watched Remi pace in that maddening dress. She stopped, swiveled on her heel, and strode back the other way.

His gaze moved to her ass, and his cock, already half hard from sitting beside her all morning, lengthened.

Fuck.

"What's taking him so long?" Remi threw her hands in the air. "Open the email, read it, open the file."

"Remi, relax."

"You relax." She huffed out a breath. "Screw it." She walked over and snatched up another sandwich. "These brie ones are so good." She ate it with a little moan.

His cock liked the sound of that, as well.

She perched on the corner of his desk. "I'm not eating any more of those, no matter how good they taste." She tapped her nails on his desk.

They were still red and sparkly, and he thought that they were a good reflection of Remi herself.

"Come on, bad guy," she muttered.

Mav studied his screen, then frowned.

"What?" She skirted the desk and leaned over him.

Her perfume hit him—something with a floral note, but not overpowering. He liked it.

"Mav?"

What was wrong with him? He didn't give a shit about perfume. He focused back on the screen. "The email was opened."

"What?" She dropped into the chair beside him. "Is the tracker picking him up?"

"No. It's not active."

Her nose scrunched up. "He didn't open the file."

"Or he has very good security that blocked our dragon angel."

She shook her head. "We designed it. Nothing can block it."

Mav fought a smile. She was like him, confident in her abilities. He liked it. There was nothing he hated more than false modesty. It was just another lie to him.

"So, we have nothing. *Argh.*" She leaped up and strode to the windows. "A big, fat *nothing.* Then when I don't hand him over the Calix file, who knows what he'll do?"

"Remi." Mav moved to her. He pressed a hand to her shoulder. "It'll be all right."

With a small sound, she pressed against his chest and hugged him.

He stilled, his arms at his sides.

She tilted her head back. "You don't hug, Rivera?"

"As a general rule, no."

"It's easy. Just put your arms around me and make soothing noises."

He frowned. "Soothing noises?"

"Like 'there, there' and 'shh.'"

He snorted and then pulled her tight against him. "I'll hug, but no soothing noises."

"Deal." She pressed her cheek to his shirt.

Damn, he realized how petite she was. The force of her personality made her seem bigger.

"You're awfully hard for a rich guy." She poked his pec.

"I work out."

"I often think I should work out more."

"How often do you do it now?"

She looked up at him, a grin on her face. "Does walking to the subway station count?"

"I don't think so."

"Then never."

Mav shook his head and fought back a laugh. This woman made him laugh and smile more than anyone he'd ever met.

"Well, I like your body just the way it is," he said.

The air changed. Worry leaked out of her eyes, replaced by heat. "Thank you. I like your body the way it is, too."

He lowered his head. Damn, it was still not enough. He wrapped an arm around her and lifted her off her feet, her body pressed tight against his.

She gasped.

"Do you like that?" he asked.

"That you can haul me up without it appearing to bother you at all?"

"Yes."

"Then the answer is yes."

"*Remi.*"

"Oh, God, and don't say my name like that." She licked her lips. "And don't look so hot."

"How do I do that?"

"I don't know. Put a paper bag over your head? Wear ugly clothes?"

He cupped her face. "Then you need to stop pulling off the impossible combination of cute and sexy."

She licked her lips again. His cock twitched, and he knew she felt it against her belly, because her eyes widened.

"Holy cow, do you have a big hard drive in your pocket?"

God, again he wanted to laugh. "No."

What the hell was it about this woman? It was like she'd cast a spell on him. Making him laugh, making him want things he'd avoided for so long.

"Actually, I don't think the paper bag will help, because I'm just as attracted to your brain."

He arched a brow. "My brain?"

"Yep." Her voice lowered. "Watching you code got me a little hot and bothered."

"Ditto," he said, voice gritty.

Her lips parted. "Mav—"

With a growl, he kissed her.

His tongue was barely in her mouth when she pulled back, staring at him.

"Oh, God, you're too hot." Her mouth slammed back against his.

The kiss was hard, wet, and deep. Hell, she tasted like sweet sin. She kissed him wildly, like she was so hungry, like she couldn't get enough.

No one had kissed him like this before.

"I wasn't...going to do this," she panted.

"Kiss me?"

"We both know it's not going to stop there, big guy."

Right now, his cock was as hard as steel. He imagined all the dirty things he wanted to do to her.

Mav backed up toward the desk.

"This is probably a *really* bad idea," she said. "Hackers from Brooklyn don't bang Manhattan billionaires."

He cocked a brow. "Says who?"

"Says everyone."

He dropped into his chair, holding Remi standing between his legs. God, she was so sexy. "I never worry about rules."

She nibbled her lip. "And I kind of like breaking them."

Mav growled and skimmed his hands up her legs, shoving her skirt up a few inches, and baring sleek thighs.

"Are you wet for me, angel?"

She nodded.

Mav leaned back. "Show me. "

"You're bossy. Is that a billionaire thing?"

"No, it's a me thing," he growled.

She reached her hands under the skirt of her dress.

"Luckily, I think it's hot," she added.

He felt that in his gut. He watched her shimmy a pair of lacy, white panties down her legs.

Fuck.

She shifted closer and he smelled the sweet, intoxicating scent of her arousal.

He pulled her to straddle him and she gasped.

"You fool around in your office much?" she gasped out.

"Never."

This small hacker seemed to bring him a lot of firsts. He slid a hand between her thighs.

She let out a long, throaty moan and Mav groaned.

She was waxed bare—all warmth and slick skin.

"My angel's wet. Damn, your thighs are slick."

He slid a finger inside her and she wasted no time writhing on his hand.

"*Maverick.*"

His thumb found her clit.

"Yes," she moaned. "Have I told you that you have great hands?"

Damn, she was hot and sexy. His gut tightened.

His computer pinged and he glanced at the screen. He kept working her, but read the message.

"Oh my God, you have your hand between my legs, and you're checking your emails?" she panted.

"Yep, told you I could multi-task." But it was damn hard to concentrate. "The Shadow didn't open the file, but I managed to get a ping. He forwarded the email to somebody else."

Remi moaned and spun, sitting back on his lap. As she read the message, she ground her hips down on his hard cock. Mav growled.

She glanced back and smiled. "Okay, back there? The message was forwarded to a guy in Manhattan called Leon Rayner."

Mav frowned.

"You know him?" she asked.

"Yeah. Young, twenty-something, from a wealthy family. Fancies himself a hacker. He's tried to get a job with me numerous times. Three, I think."

"Hmm. You think he got mixed up with The Shadow?"

"It's a strong possibility."

"He might know who The Shadow is. We could infect his phone with our dragon angel."

Mav smiled. "That's an excellent idea."

She leaned back, her mouth on his neck. "Now, where were you?"

He kept his hand between her legs, stroking. She looked delectable sprawled over his lap. His fingers found her clit again, and he worked it. She writhed.

"*Mav.*"

"I like the way you breathe my name, Remi."

She moved, and their mouths collided. She kissed him, tongues tangling as he flicked her clit. A second later, she came.

Mav swallowed her cries. He wanted to do more, but this was his office, and it wasn't the place.

She sagged against him, face flushed. "Mav."

"Shh." He pulled her dress down. His control was shredded, and his hands weren't steady. "Later."

She licked her lips. "Okay."

Making himself focus, he tapped the screen.

A picture of a young, well-groomed man popped up.

"Rayner will be at a gala event tonight. To raise money for inner-city schools. Keen to drink some excellent champagne, and eat some tasty canapés?"

"I guess I could grin and bear it." She nuzzled his neck, reminding him of a sleek, satisfied cat. "I thought you didn't like parties?"

"I hate them. But uploading a trojan on to Rayner's phone should make it more interesting."

She smiled. "I'm one-hundred-percent in agreement."

And Mav suspected having Remi there with him would make it more bearable.

9

HE DOESN'T EVEN NEED A LINE

Remi

I finished doing my makeup and stepped back.

Wow, I looked amazing. Sexy, hot, and gorgeous.

My little loft didn't do my stunning dress justice. Mav had told me he'd have a dress delivered, and when the bag arrived, I never imagined anything like this. I fingered the silky blue fabric. It looked expensive, felt expensive, hell, it smelled expensive.

The dress fit me like a glove. It had a deep V that showed off major cleavage, then hugged my curves before flaring to the floor. It was a gorgeous, rich blue.

He'd sent jewelry as well. Thankfully not a big pile of diamonds, which would've given me a heart attack. The funky, statement necklace was made of twists of gold. I slid matching twists into my ears. The color looked good on my skin.

I stilled. Surely it wasn't real gold. I fingered it. But it probably was, wasn't it?

My phone beeped.

Car is on the way to get you.

I could practically hear his deep voice. And the things he'd whispered to me in his office. *You wet for me angel? I like the way you breathe my name, Remi.*

I shivered. I was turned on. The man was all the way over in Manhattan, and my panties were wet.

I closed my eyes. I'd fooled around with Maverick Rivera. He'd made me come on his hand.

And I'd liked it.

I wanted to do it again.

Crap. I needed my head in the game. I straightened. I needed to get our little dragon angel onto Rayner's phone.

After that, we'd see about this thing with Mav. I really wanted to get the man out of his tuxedo.

I could do this, right? I could have a hot little hook-up with him, and keep it simple and uncomplicated.

I looked into the mirror.

Man, I totally sucked at lying to myself.

I heard the honk of a horn outside and grabbed the black evening bag. I shoved my phone, lipstick, and wallet inside. I grabbed my black, evening cape and slipped it on.

When the dress had arrived, I'd taken the time to paint my nails to match. They were now the same deep blue, with little gold jewels on some of them.

I headed down the stairs carefully in my heels. I paused. There was no sound in the workshop. Steve would be at home with Kaylee.

I snuck out of the garage.

And spotted a huge, black limo on the street.

My jaw dropped open. *Holy cow*.

I hustled toward it.

A door opened behind me.

"Remi?"

At the sound of Mama's voice, I winced and spun.

She stood in her doorway, looking down at me. Her eyes widened, taking in my dress, then the limo.

"Um, I have a work thing in Manhattan."

Her brows rose. "A work thing?"

"Yes."

"Remi, I know when you're lying, child."

"I'm not lying." *Just not telling you the entire truth*.

"You're all right?"

I walked up the stairs and took her hands. "Yes, I'm all right."

She studied me a long time. "Okay." Her face softened. "You look beautiful."

I smiled. "I feel beautiful."

Mama smiled. "I'm sure he'll think so, too."

"Who?"

"Whoever the man is who's put that twinkle in your eye."

"Mama, a woman doesn't need a man for that."

"Pfft, only a special someone who gets the juices flowing can put that look on a woman's face."

I winced. "I am not talking about any sort of flowing juices with you."

She kissed my cheek. "Go. Have fun."

I hurried to the limo, and the driver held the door open for me and nodded.

I wasn't off to have fun. I was off to hack Rayner, so we could track The Shadow, and ultimately, I could save Mama.

I fidgeted as we drove. The limo was gorgeous—buttery-leather seats, spacious and luxurious.

I heard the driver make a call in front. He had an earpiece in his ear.

"Yes, sir, we're en route." A pause. "Yes, she's wearing the dress."

I looked out the window and smiled.

When we finally pulled up, I saw the Queensboro Bridge and a crowd.

Oh, I hadn't thought to ask where the event was. I figured it would be at some fancy hotel ballroom.

This was Guastavino's.

It was a New York City landmark. Tucked in under the bridge, it had a famous, tiled, vaulted ceiling. It was a favorite location for events and weddings.

The driver helped me out and I dragged in a deep breath.

I saw a line of people moving inside the glass doors. Urns taller than me were filled with cherry blossoms.

I lifted my chin. All around me were men in tuxedos, and women in designer dresses.

No one knows that you don't belong, Remi.

Despite the seriousness of the night, I was going to enjoy it. I showed the invite Mav had sent with the dress, and then I was in.

I checked my cape and walked into the main room.

"Oh, wow."

The vaulted, tile ceiling was beautiful and unique.

The space was filled with large, round tables, with giant centerpieces filled with more elegant cherry blossoms. The entire place was lit up with pale-pink light.

It looked like a dream.

An expensive, elegant dream.

"Champagne, miss?" A server in a white suit stopped in front of me, holding a tray of champagne flutes.

"Hell, yes." I took a flute and sipped. *Yum.*

I wandered the crowd. I saw a few faces I recognized —politicians, actors, models, well-known business people. The Who's Who of the wealthy and famous of New York.

Where the hell was Mav?

I wandered some more. A man smiled at me. He was handsome, and looked good in his tux. I gave him a polite smile and kept moving.

"A beautiful woman I haven't met. I just had to rectify the situation."

I turned. This one was handsome, too. Clean-cut man, blond, cute face.

"Does that line work for you a lot?" I asked.

He smiled. "Fifty-fifty."

Then I felt a prickle on the back of my neck.

The man glanced past me, and his smile slipped. I looked back, and everything in me clenched with need.

Mav stalked toward me. Everything about him was dark—a black tux with a black shirt, and a black scowl.

My pulse skidded, then raced.

I glanced back at the blond man. "Keep practicing. He doesn't even need a line."

I turned to face my incoming dragon.

He stopped an inch from me, his hot gaze sliding down, then up.

"Who was the guy?" he growled.

"What guy?" I knew people were watching us. I straightened his bowtie. "Good evening to you, too. Why, thank you, I think the dress looks great, too. And you look hot in a tux."

He growled again, then yanked me close and kissed me.

Mav

Mav lifted Remi off her feet, his mouth taking hers hard.

There wasn't much to her, so it was easy to hold her pinned against him. She made a hungry sound, and kissed him back. Giving as good as she got.

Coming to his senses, Mav lifted his head. He saw fierce hunger in her eyes. A ferocious, possessive need rose up in him. He was a loyal friend, protective of his family, but he'd never felt like this about a woman. Not even Hannah.

"Way to keep a low profile, big guy."

He set her down, well aware that people were looking, whispering.

"People always watch me." He hated it. "When I'm not doing anything interesting, they make stuff up."

"So, you figured you'd give them something to gossip about." She slipped her arm through his.

"Actually, I wasn't thinking about anything but you."

She stilled.

Crap. He hadn't meant to say that. The words had just slipped out. That seemed to happen a lot around Remi.

She went up on her toes and pressed a quick kiss to his lips.

"I need more champagne." They walked across the room.

"Have you seen Rayner?" he asked.

"No."

"Too busy getting accosted by jackasses?"

"He had a tired pickup line. If you wanted no one to notice me, you shouldn't have given me this dress."

Mav grunted. He wanted to burn the dress. "I'll cover you in a sack."

She grinned.

He got her another champagne, and she sipped it.

"I love the jewelry," she said.

His gaze dropped to the necklace. It succeeded in dragging his gaze to her luscious, full breasts.

Yes. Burning the dress *and* the jewelry.

"It's not real gold, right?" She stroked the necklace and he noticed that her nails were now blue.

He arched a brow.

"Right. Don't tell me."

"I saw the necklace and earrings. I thought you'd like them."

And he'd wanted to see them on her. Preferably while naked.

"I need a drink," he growled.

She held out her glass.

"No, I need a scotch."

"Well, I—" she broke off, looking behind him.

"Remi?"

She leaned in, pressing her palms to Mav's chest. "It's Rayner."

Mav straightened. He slipped a hand in the pocket of his trousers, and touched his phone.

"Ready?" she murmured.

He nodded. He leaned down, his mouth brushing hers.

"The phone is set to transmit. We just need to get close enough."

She cocked her head, looking like a feisty princess, ready to defend her realm.

He scowled. Jeez, where was his brain coming up with this stuff?

They wandered closer. He saw Leon Rayner now. The man wore his tuxedo with ease, and had the rich, entitled look that some kids from wealthy families got.

"Canapé?" Mav swung Remi close to the table loaded with food.

"Sure thing." She popped something in her mouth. Her face changed.

He worked hard not to laugh. "Not to your liking, angel?"

She swallowed and her nose wrinkled. Then she drained her champagne flute.

"*Ugh*. That was disgusting."

Mav laughed quietly.

"Quit it." She hit his chest.

"Maverick Rivera. A pleasure."

Mav straightened and faced Rayner. He was a shade under six feet, slim, elegant.

The man smiled. "It's nice to see you."

"It's Rayner, right?" Mav said.

The man's smile dimmed. "Right."

Mav lifted his chin. *Just a little closer.*

"How are things at Rivera Tech?"

"Busy. We always have new projects on the boil."

"He's *always* so busy." Remi leaned in with a bright smile.

Rayner's smile widened. "I don't think we've met. I'm Leon Rayner."

"This is Angelica." Mav pulled her closer.

"I've been busy myself," Rayner said. "I have lots of work going on."

"Leon!" A trio of men nearby called out to the man.

"Excuse me. A pleasure to meet you, Angelica." With a nod, he walked away.

Dammit. Mav pulled his phone out. "Fuck."

"Not long enough?"

He shook his head.

"Give it to me." She took the phone. "Now look angry, say something nasty, and stride off to get that scotch."

Maverick glowered. "I hate that every man here has a perfect view of your breasts."

"Wow." She put a hurt look on her face. "You're so good at grumpy and snarly."

"So I'm told." He leaned over her, glaring.

"And need I remind you that you picked the dress? I think my breasts look great."

111

"They do. They look very good." He swiveled and strode off.

He headed to the bar, hating that he was leaving her alone. He reached the bar and the bartender headed over.

"Scotch. Neat. The best you have."

The bartender nodded and turned away. Mav leaned on the bar and glanced in Remi's direction.

She was convincingly wiping her eyes. A second later, Rayner appeared, talking to her. Remi shook her head, and offered him a watery smile.

Rayner sidled closer.

Mav frowned. The asshole didn't need to get that close.

Remi took his arm, and angled in closer, her breast brushing against Rayner's arm.

Damn, she was good. The phone was practically rubbing the guy.

"Your drink, sir."

He took it and drained it in one gulp. He watched Remi smiling, flirting.

A second later, she looked at her watch, then beamed at Rayner, patted his arm, and walked away.

Mav didn't miss all the other sets of male eyes watching her.

As she got closer, she caught Mav's gaze, winked, then walked out of Guastavino's.

A beat later, Mav followed.

Outside, a few people milled around. Late arrivals were coming in, others braving the cold to smoke, or escape the crowd inside.

Remi turned, now with a high-necked, black cape around her, and a grin trained up at him. "Uploaded."

Mav scooped her up and she wrapped her legs around his waist.

"You are good," he said.

"Oh, I know, big guy, I know." She kissed him.

Fuck. Every time he kissed her, he thought this gut-gnawing need would lessen.

It only got worse.

"I like working with you," she said. "Right now, that little trojan of ours is doing its thing."

It was a hell of a feeling.

"Well, well, well," an amused male voice drawled.

Shit. Mav turned his head.

Beside him, Zane stood with Monroe. The woman's dark hair was up, and she was wearing a sleek, aquamarine dress, peeking out from under a black evening coat.

Beside them, a grinning Liam looked impeccable in his tuxedo and overcoat, and Aspen wore a blush-pink dress with a fitted top covered in silver beads, and a long full skirt. She had a furry, silvery-white bolero coat over her shoulders and arms.

Mav set Remi on her feet.

"Maverick Rivera kissing a woman in public." Zane looked at Liam. "He ever been into PDA?"

"No."

Monroe elbowed Zane. "Who's your friend, Mav?"

"Hi." Remi gave a little wave. "I'm Remi."

Mav watched his friends study her.

"It's a pleasure to meet you, Remi," Zane said, all charm. "How do you know Mav?"

"Oh, well, I...work with computers."

His friends weren't dumb. They were very sharp, and they'd used their brains to make themselves billions of dollars. He could see them putting things together.

"We have to go," Mav said.

"But we just got here," Aspen said.

"I need to get Remi home."

"Remi." Zane pinned her with a glare. "You wouldn't happen to be a hacker, would you?"

Remi lifted her chin. "That's none of your business, Mr. Roth," she said sweetly.

Both Zane and Liam turned to Mav.

"Mav, what the hell?" Zane snapped. "She's a *traitor*."

Mav felt Remi flinch.

"Zane—"

"Mav, you fought hard to protect us when you thought we needed it. Now it's our turn." Zane shot Remi a dark look. "I won't let her drag you down. Not like Hannah did."

"I'm handling this," Mav said.

"By kissing the hell out of your hacker? Is that your plan?"

"*Zane*," Mav growled.

"She can't hurt you if she's locked up in jail."

Remi gasped.

Mav slid his arm around her. "Enough. There are things you don't understand." He saw Remi shiver from the cold.

He stripped off his jacket and draped it over her shoulders.

"I can't explain everything to you yet. I need you to trust me."

His friends looked away, jaws tight. Monroe and Aspen looked worried.

"I need to get Remi home."

"Mav, tread carefully," Zane warned. "Treason is treason."

Mav nodded, then whisked Remi toward the limo.

"Will they...have me arrested?" she asked.

"No. That's not going to happen." The euphoria of the night was ruined. "Let's get you home."

10

MY EYES ARE WIDE OPEN

Remi

I sat in the back of the limo, my belly churning.

Mav sat beside me, brooding. His dark mood filled the vehicle.

"Your friends are...very protective."

"They've both been through some situations lately. Both have fallen in love."

"I read about some of it. Two billionaire bachelors off the market is big news." I fiddled with my fingers in my lap. "You're lucky to have friends like that."

He took my hand. "When this is over, when it's safe, I'll explain it to them. You aren't a traitor, Remi."

"Thanks to you. If I'd kept my blinders on..." I shivered.

"But you didn't."

I dragged in a breath. "Who's Hannah?"

He stiffened, sending a fierce scowl at his shoes.

I slipped my hand free. "Sorry. None of my business."

Dark eyes met mine, churning.

My belly clutched.

"Met her in college. Fell for her."

Ugh. I felt claws in my belly and looked out the window. I hated the idea of Mav falling for anyone.

I couldn't stop myself from looking back.

"She was tall, blonde, pretty, smart," he said.

Okay, now I really, *really* hated Miss Perky Hannah. "What happened?" I whispered.

"She was a fake. A fraud. I'd just sold a computer chip. My first big deal."

"You were about to make a lot of money."

"Yeah." A muscle ticked in his jaw. "I noticed her slipping out to make a few calls. Being cagey about messages." He made a harsh sound. "I was worried she was cheating on me. They were messages from her father."

"You hacked her phone."

He nodded. "Her father owned a chain of electronics stores. He was on the verge of bankruptcy and had engineered all of it. For her to run into me at a party. To be the perfect, attentive girlfriend. She even had this guy from before me. She told me they were just friends, but I think it was more. She was a liar, a fraud."

"Did she explain?"

"I didn't give her the chance. She was crying, pleading, she was sorry—" He shook his head. "She taught me a lesson."

Oh, Mav. That woman had hurt him, scarred him.

And he'd shown me that part of himself.

Ignoring all the warning alarms that I was getting in way too deep I shifted closer.

"One of my first foster homes—" I cleared my throat "—it was nice. I liked the parents. They had a daughter a few years older than me. She did my hair, gave me candy, told me that we would be sisters."

A dark look settled on his face and he entwined our fingers.

"But in our bedroom, she'd turn nasty. She'd pinch and scratch me where it wouldn't show. Under my shirt, I was a mass of bruises. She told me I wasn't her real sister, that I was trash. My parents didn't want me, and they threw me away like trash."

"That's *nothing* to do with you. She was mean, and probably had her own issues."

"I know. Mama helped me realize that." Remi leaned closer. "And Hannah had her own issues, too. They were nothing to do with you. You were just a pawn that got caught in her mess."

Something flickered in his eyes. He brushed his nose against hers. "I really want to kiss you right now."

"I really want you to kiss me right now."

He slid a hand into her hair. "But I'm not going to, or I'll end up tearing that dress off you and fucking you on this seat."

My womb spasmed. "Um, again, I'm totally on board."

He growled. I loved that sound.

"We just turned onto your street."

Dammit. The limo stopped and a second later, I saw

the curtains in the house twitch. Mama had been waiting for me.

Mav's fingers stroked my skin. "I need to get home and see what our dragon angel is doing. This is our one chance to find The Shadow and stop him."

I nodded, trying to get my hormones under control. *Damn hormones.*

Mav opened the door and stepped out. He helped me out of the limo.

"I'll walk you to the door," he said.

A billionaire walking me to the door of an auto shop. I felt a giggle welling.

I pulled out my key, and when I heard a throat clear, I turned.

Mama, with her arms crossed, was standing at her gate.

"Evening, Mama."

Her gaze was on Mav. "Did you have a good evening?"

"Yes. Mama, this is Maverick. Mav, this is Mama Alma."

"A pleasure to meet you." He held out a hand. "Remi speaks very highly of you."

Mama shook his hand, studying him like he was a bug. "I hope you're treating my girl right, Maverick."

He smiled, his teeth white in the darkness. "Remi wouldn't let me get away with it, if I didn't."

Mama smiled. "That is very true."

"Um...I'd better head up," I said.

Mav turned back toward me and our gazes locked.

"Good night, Remi."

"Night, Mav." I handed back his jacket.

He strode back to the limo and I watched his powerful stride. Okay, I watched his ass.

He slid into the car with a wave, and the limo prowled off down the street.

"What are you doing, child?"

Without the added warmth of Mav's jacket, the chilly night air crept under my cape. I turned to Mama. "We're working together."

She made a sound. "I'm old, not dead. He doesn't look at you like it's work, and I saw you eyeing that boy's mighty fine ass."

I took half a second to marvel that she'd called Maverick Rivera a boy.

"He's a billionaire, Remi. He's different, and billionaires do as they please, with whomever they please, and then move on."

That was nothing I hadn't already told myself.

"You don't know him, Mama. And I know. My eyes are wide open."

"I know, child." She cupped my cheek. "You've always been so smart, but also so hungry for love. Like a sponge. A prickly one, but still a sponge, ready to soak it up."

"I...I won't fall in love with him."

I couldn't afford that heartache.

Mama made a harrumphing sound. "I'm tired. Time for bed."

I kissed her cheek. "Night, Mama. Love you."

"I love you, too."

I watched her carefully negotiate the stairs.

"You were the first person I loved," I told her.

She turned. "It's an honor. Now don't make me cry, or no cookies for you tomorrow."

With a smile, I headed inside and up to my loft.

I shed my dress, hanging it up, then carefully set the jewelry aside. I pulled on my red-plaid pajama bottoms and a fitted, long-sleeved, black top.

Ah, it was so good to ditch the bra and heels.

I loosened my hair, and took my time washing my makeup off.

I was thinking of Mav as I drifted off to sleep.

Remi

I woke in the pitch blackness, and blinked.

Frowning, I rolled and looked to the glow of the bedside clock through the gauzy curtain around my bed.

2:05 AM.

With a groan, I flopped back on my pillow. I'd only been asleep a few hours. I wondered what had woken me?

I didn't remember any X-rated dreams starring a certain tech billionaire. Dragging in a breath, I rolled over.

Then I frowned.

I smelled smoke.

I sat up and sniffed again. It wasn't super strong, but it was definitely noticeable.

Reaching over, I turned on my bedside lamp, then

slipped on a comfy pair of running shoes, and my favorite knit cardigan. Habit had me sliding my phone into my pocket.

Heading down the stairs, I sniffed. Nothing seemed amiss in Steve's workshop.

Then I heard shouts from outside, and my pulse spiked.

Rushing to the door, I yanked it open. Horror hit me like a tidal wave.

Mama's house was on fire.

I saw flames. I saw smoke.

"Mama!" *God, the kids.*

I ran to the front door and banged on it. "Mama!"

That's when I saw the chain and padlock, and my chest froze. Someone had *locked* the door shut.

No. No!

I raced to Steve's basement apartment. "Steve!" God, it was locked shut, too.

Panic and fear were hot and slick in my veins.

"Remi!" Steve's muffled shout. "I can smell smoke. The door's blocked. We can't get out."

What did I do?

"Hold on," I shouted.

I raced back up and saw windows open above. Charlie's terrified face looked down at me.

"Remi! There's a fire."

"I know, Charlie. Hold on. I'll get you out."

I yanked my phone out, hand shaking.

"Remi?" Mav's sleep-gritty voice.

"Mav, oh, God."

"What's wrong?" He sounded alert.

"Mama's house is on fire! The doors are chained shut. Mav—"

"Stay calm. I'm on my way. I'll call 9-1-1. Remi, go and get Boone."

"Who?" I couldn't think.

"My man across the street."

"Oh, right."

"Do *not* go in that building, Remi. I'm coming."

I shoved the phone in my pocket, and darted across the street. Lights were coming on in the surrounding houses, and people were coming out.

"Call 9-1-1," I yelled.

I raced to the door of Mrs. Hansen's house. Before I thumped my fist on it, the door was yanked open.

A wall of muscled, shirtless chest greeted me. The guy was ripped, and held a pistol at his side. His rugged face looked grim.

"The house is on fire," I yelled. "The doors have been chained shut."

He glanced past me and muttered a curse.

He shoved the gun in the back of his jeans, then swiveled. He was back a second later, shrugging a plaid shirt on. He had bolt cutters, and an axe in his hands.

We raced back to the house.

I looked up—Charlie, Jamal, and Naomi were at the windows, coughing and crying.

Boone thundered down to Steve's basement.

"Hold on!" I yelled at the kids.

"The fire is in here," Jamal screamed.

Boone returned a second later. Steve staggered behind him, clutching a hysterical Kaylee in his arms.

Boone positioned himself under the window, legs braced. "Jump, kid."

Jamal's eyes went wide.

"We've got you," I cried. "Come on." I moved in close to Boone and waved.

"Go on, Jamal," Naomi said.

Jamal threw his skinny legs over the window sill. He was in a pair of blue pajamas.

He jumped.

Boone caught him and handed him off to me.

"Come on." Boone waved at Charlie next.

The little boy leaped.

Boone caught him as well.

Naomi hesitated.

"You can do this, Naomi," I said.

She pulled in a shuddering breath and jumped. Boone caught her, going back a step.

I raced to her, hugging her tight. "Come and sit with the boys on the sidewalk. You're fine. It'll be fine."

"Mama?" Naomi said, tears tracking down her cheeks.

"We'll get her." I fought my own fear and looked at Boone. "Our mother is inside."

Boone nodded. He took the bolt cutters and put them against the chain on the door.

Snap.

He yanked the door open, and flames and smoke roared out.

Boone shoved me to the side.

"Where's her room?" he demanded.

God, how could anyone survive this?

"Remi," Boone barked. "Where's her room?"

"Upstairs." Tears ran down my face. "Back left. Here." I shrugged off my cardigan.

He pulled the garment over his head, and disappeared into the inferno.

God. *God*. She had to be all right.

I wanted to help. But I took one step into the doorway, and it was like entering the gates of hell.

Sirens cut through the night, and a fire engine screamed down the street.

I moved over to the kids, hugging them.

The truck screeched to a halt, and soon, firefighters streamed around, shouting orders.

"Anyone inside?" one of them yelled.

"Our mother," I said. "And our neighbor went to get her."

"Get the hoses going," the man yelled. "We've got two people inside, and we need to stop it before she spreads."

I kept my gaze on the door. *Please, please*.

Somewhere, a window shattered.

Onlookers screamed.

"*Remi*." Charlie grabbed me, clenching hard.

I patted his back. "It'll be okay."

He let go and Naomi grabbed him.

A sleek sports car sped down the street and slammed to a halt. When I saw Mav's tall form leap out, something inside me clenched tight.

He shoved past the firefighters; his gaze locked on me.

"*Mav*."

He lifted me off my feet and I wrapped myself around him. He was so big, so strong.

"Mama's still inside—" my voice cracked "—and Boone's in there."

"Jesus." Mav held me tight.

We stared at the door. *Please, please.*

Suddenly, a big form staggered out the door, something held in its arms.

"Oh, my God," I cried.

Mav let me go and he raced forward, as Boone broke into a hacking cough.

"We need help!" Mav roared. He took Mama from Boone.

I grabbed Boone, leaning into his side. He kept coughing. I took some of his weight, and nearly staggered.

Ahead, I saw Mav put Mama on a stretcher. Paramedics rushed around her.

She was so still.

Then a firefighter and another paramedic took Boone.

"I'm fine." The man coughed again.

"Dude, we're putting a mask on you." The paramedic was a tall, broad, bald, African-American man. "Don't make me get rough."

Boone gave a reluctant nod.

Mav returned, his arms wrapping around me.

"God, Mav." I pushed my hair back. "Someone chained the doors closed. *God.*"

My phone vibrated. I almost ignored it, but I pulled it out.

An email from The Shadow.

It was a picture of Mav and me, kissing at Guastavino's.

"No." Nausea welled. "It was The Shadow. *He* did this."

Mav cursed and tipped his chin up. "It's going to be okay."

"How is this okay?" I whispered.

"I'll protect you and your family, Remi. I promise."

11

PANCAKES

Mav

Mav tried to control the rage vibrating inside him.

He held Remi tight to him as she spoke to the frightened kids. He kissed the top of her head. "I need to make some calls."

Mav called his head of security, and shot a text off to Vander Norcross. The man owned a security firm in San Francisco and had recommended Boone. He was former military, an all-round badass, and he'd helped out both Zane and Liam.

Boone appeared.

"Shouldn't you be in an ambulance?" Mav asked.

The man grunted. "I'm fine. And if that paramedic comes near me with that mask again…"

"Thank you," Mav said.

Another grunt. The former soldier scowled at the building. The firefighters almost had the blaze under control.

"I should've caught it sooner."

"It's two-thirty in the morning, Boone. You were here. You helped Remi and her family. This is The Shadow's doing. He sent Remi a picture of the two of us."

"Punishment." A muscle in Boone's jaw tightened. "The guy knows she's working with you."

"Yeah. I made some calls. I'm going to put her family in a safe house upstate, with security, until this is over. Can you go with them? Be in charge of the team?"

Boone's gaze darkened. "I work better alone." He looked to where Remi was holding the little blonde girl on her hip. "But yeah, I'll do it. What about Remi?"

"She'll be staying with me."

A faint smile slipped across Boone's face. "I figured as much."

Remi had moved over to check on Mama. The woman was now conscious, resting on the stretcher with a mask on.

Mav joined them.

"Mav." Remi pressed her face to his chest and he ran a hand up her back. "She's going to be all right." There were tears in Remi's eyes.

Mav saw how Mama was watching them.

"Remi, I want to send your family to a safe place. A nice house, upstate. I'm going to send Boone and a security team with them."

She bit her lip. "It's too much—"

"No. The Shadow did this. I promised you that I'd keep them safe." He cupped her face. "Keep you safe."

"Thank you." She nibbled her lip. "Boone will stay with them?"

"Yes."

She nodded. "Okay."

Boone stepped closer. "I'll go with Mama to the hospital, and take her to the safe house when she's released."

Mav nodded. "And I have a team en route to collect your brother and the kids."

Remi nodded tiredly.

"You're staying with me," Mav added.

She met his gaze for a long beat. "Okay."

Over the next thirty minutes, Mav dealt with the cops and firefighters. Remi hugged all the kids and helped load them into a black van that had arrived, driven by Mav's security team.

She had an intense conversation with Steve before the family left.

"Get your things," Mav said.

He followed her up the stairs to her loft. He eyed her small space, liking the industrial vibe, and all the color.

Pure Remi.

She packed a small suitcase, and then put her laptop into a bag. She looked exhausted; her face was smeared with soot.

"Come on, angel." He led her out to his car.

She was silent on the ride to his place. He turned onto his street.

"You live in SoHo?" she said.

"Yes."

He pulled into the garage of his building and grabbed her bags. She looked around. He pressed a button for the elevator.

She eyed him. "I thought you'd go for sleek and modern."

"I'll show you Zane's place sometime." Mav shrugged. "I like a little history. I like this place. It's solid, sturdy. I like the cast iron buildings in SoHo. This one dates from the late 1800s."

They stepped into the elevator. He touched the button for the fifth floor of the seven-story building.

"Do you own the entire building?"

"Yes, but only live on the top three floors. The rest is rented."

"Only three floors. Got it."

"I hear that sarcasm."

The doors opened into his living area, and her lips parted. She walked in, taking in the brick walls that had been painted white, contrasting with the black frames around the windows. She wandered to the black-tile fireplace.

"This is the Great Room," he said. "Or at least that's what the designer called it."

She looked up at the skylights. "It must be drenched with light during the day."

He nodded.

She wandered into the kitchen and gasped. "Naomi would *love* this. Wow." She turned taking in the gray, floor-to-ceiling cabinets, the enormous island topped with black stone.

On the other side of a long, rustic table was another fireplace. She glanced out to the terrace—there was an outdoor table, and chairs clustered around the outdoor fireplace.

"How many terraces?" she asked.

"Six."

"Jeez."

"Come on. I bet you'd like a shower."

She nodded, not bothering to hide her desire for that.

They headed up the oval-shaped staircase, also in black. He saw her taking it all in. Strangely, he felt nervous. He wanted her to like it.

She paused at a window. It gave a perfect view of the cobblestone, SoHo street below, and the row of historic buildings lining it.

He hadn't wanted to be on top of a skyscraper. He hadn't wanted his home to feel like a hotel.

"I like your place, Mav. It feels like home."

Warmth filled him. He led her into his bedroom.

She scanned the huge, gray bed, the gray walls, and the large rug and two comfy armchairs arranged in front of the fireplace.

She smiled and pointed. "You brood here, right? In front of the fireplace."

He set her bags down and slapped her ass. He was glad to see her smiling. "I don't brood."

She snorted.

"Get in the shower. I'll make you some tea, or something."

"Tea? Do you know how to make tea?"

"How hard can it be? Hot water and tea leaves."

She snorted again.

"I see your sass is returning."

She met his gaze. "Because I feel safe. And I know my family is safe." She swallowed. "Thank you, Mav."

He felt itchy. "It's nothing."

"Not to me. To me it's something." Her face hardened. "The Shadow tried to kill my family." The words exploded out of her. She threw her arms up. "God, that *asshole*."

"Hey." Mav took her hand. "Your family is fine."

"I'm going to make The Shadow pay. For this, for whatever he has planned. You and I will track him down and skewer the prick."

"I like you bloodthirsty." It beat shell-shocked and worried. "Now, go and clean the soot off. You hungry?"

"Mav, it's four AM."

"So?" He often stayed up working late, and ate at odd hours.

"Can you even cook?" she asked.

"I'll try not to kill us."

With a smile, she wandered into his bathroom. He heard her moan. "Look at this marble. And this bath tub."

Smiling, Mav headed to the kitchen, fighting the knowledge that she was in his bathroom and taking her clothes off.

He blew out a breath. She was hurt. Upset. He wouldn't take advantage.

It might kill him, but he'd take care of her, and nothing else.

Remi

I stepped out of Mav's amazing shower.

The guy didn't only have one, he had *two* showers in the master bathroom.

I dried off, so glad to be warm and clean. As I wrapped the towel around my wet hair, I spotted a fluffy, white robe hanging off a nearby hook and slipped it on.

It was way too big for me. Robes always were. They were not designed for short people. I stared at the tub and imagined lounging in it. It was set in front of huge, floor-to-ceiling windows that looked onto a small terrace ringed by greenery. No one would be able to see in.

I swiveled and looked at myself in the mirror. I looked like I was thirteen.

Oh, well. Mav had seen me dressed up, covered in soot and tears, and now makeup-free.

I hoped Mama and the others were okay. I pulled in a deep breath. I would make The Shadow regret this.

I tightened the belt on the robe and then tied my hair up. Then I went to find Mav.

Quietly, I padded downstairs. I *loved* his place. It made my loft look like a closet. I heard him in the kitchen, and paused in the doorway.

There was something about seeing a man, especially a big, muscular one, in the kitchen. He set a steaming mug down on the island, then turned back to the frypan on a giant, shiny stove. He was making pancakes.

"I love pancakes."

He glanced over his shoulder and took in the robe, something hungry lurking in his gaze.

"Your tea." He jerked his head. "Pancakes are nearly ready."

I sat on a stool at the island, rearranging the robe to cover my legs. "Did your mom teach you to cook?"

"Yes. She swore her kids, boys included, would cook. I'm no chef, but I don't starve."

I sipped my tea. It was soothing. "But you'd prefer to be in your lab."

"Yeah."

"Do you have a lab here?"

"No, I'd work twenty-four hours a day, if I did. I have a home office, and a decent home computer system. After the pancakes, I'll show you."

"Ooh, the big, bad tech billionaire wants to impress me with his system."

His lips quirked.

I loved every little smile I earned from this man.

He set a plate of pancakes down in front of me, and I found that I was ravenous. I tipped maple syrup liberally over mine, and Mav ate his standing up.

A phone dinged and I glanced sideways. I saw my phone resting on the counter.

"I got it out of your bag," Mav said.

My belly curdled. It was a message from The Shadow.

I don't take a double-cross lightly.

There was another picture of Mav and I attached.

"Fuck off." I started typing.

"Remi—"

I shook my head.

Asshole. You tried to kill my family. You made an
ENEMY .

There was no response.

I leaped off my stool and paced. "Who just tries to kill innocent people?"

"Bad guys."

I turned and almost ran into Mav.

"I'm so *angry*."

He took my hand and squeezed. "And together, we'll make him pay."

I nodded.

"Come on."

He led me out of the kitchen and down the hall.

And into an office.

I gasped. "Oh my God."

The room was a hacker's wet dream. There were screens all over the wall, and a curved desk, with two gamer chairs.

"Computer, grant system access to Remi Solano."

"Please place your hand on the scanner," a modulated, female voice said. "Initiate voice sample."

"Is that the voice of the *Star Trek* computer?" I asked.

Mav nodded at me.

"Cool."

"Say your name." He pointed at a scanner pad on the desk.

"Uh, Remi Solano." I put my hand on the scanner and it flashed.

"Access granted," the computer said.

The screens displayed his security feeds. I saw all his

windows and doors had pressure sensors, that showed up on the schematics for his home-security system.

He lived in a high-tech castle.

I spied the computer unit beneath the desk.

"Mav, what is that?"

"An Ultra600."

My pulse raced. "But you've only got 300s on the market."

He smiled. "This is an experimental prototype. I own the company, remember?"

I sat down and tapped on the keyboard. "This is *beautiful*." I cruised through his system.

Mav leaned against the desk. "Hello? Remember me?"

I rolled my eyes. "How's the tracker that we put on Rayner?"

He leaned over and touched the keyboard.

I studied the info and frowned. "He hasn't made contact with The Shadow yet. Damn."

"He will. We just need to be patient."

I thought of Mama, the burning house, Steve missing work, the kids uprooted and missing school.

Dammit. I didn't want to be patient. I wanted The Shadow to pay, and for this to be over.

Mav's phone chimed. "Message from Boone. Everyone is fine. They're all at the safe house, and the kids are mowing into McDonald's breakfast. Mama is resting comfortably."

I released a long breath. "I can never thank you enough, Mav."

"You don't need to." He turned away.

"Hey." I grabbed his arm. "Don't be grumpy. You're doing a good thing. Accept my thanks."

"Fine."

His scowl made me smile. "So gracious."

"It's been a rough night. We should grab some sleep."

I snorted. "There is *no* way I could sleep now."

"TV?"

I cocked my head. "Have you got some games on this fancy computer?" I dropped into the chair.

"Yes, although I have a game console in my movie room."

"Of course, you have a movie room. No, let's play here." She smiled. "We can make another bet."

He sat and arched a brow.

"If you win, do you still want that kiss?" she asked.

I saw the struggle on his face. My gut turned sour. Had he changed his mind about wanting me? Had all this killed his desire?

"Remi..." he said carefully. "You've had a bad night. Your family was hurt and threatened. That's a lot to deal with, and I won't take advantage of you."

I studied his rugged face, his strong jaw. "You're being noble."

His scowl deepened. "No, I'm not. I'm just not being an asshole."

"Actually, I don't seem to mind when you're an asshole."

His gaze fastened on me. I scooted my chair closer.

"I just kind of like you as you are. So, let's game. If you win, you get a kiss." I crossed my legs and the robe parted. *Oops.* I accidentally showed off a lot of thigh. His gaze jerked down.

"What are you wearing under that?" he growled.

"Absolutely nothing."

He growled again, his hot gaze back on my face. My belly felt alive with flames.

"If I win," I said. "I'm going to fuck your brains out, right here in that chair. Deal?"

12

MY ANGEL

Mav

He could smell her fresh, clean scent. She watched him with that maddening smile—like she knew a joke that he didn't. Her legs weren't long, but her skin was smooth, her legs shapely.

He wanted her.

Desperately.

More than he'd wanted any woman. Hell, anything.

How had this happened? How after years of guarding himself, had this small hacker slid through his defenses with such ease?

Remi made him think of catching a firefly in a jar. Holding all that light and energy in the palm of your hand.

He clamped his hands on the arms of his chair.

"I'm trying to do the right thing here," he said.

She rose. "I get to decide what's right for me. I spent my

childhood having well-meaning people dictate my life. Now, I choose what's best for me." Her robe parted, showing him her naked body beneath. Petite, curvy, and luscious.

His cock swelled, pressing hard against his zipper.

"Remi—"

She pressed her hands over his, and leaned closer. He saw her breasts sway, topped by pink nipples.

"I know what I want," she said.

That sexy whisper rocketed through him. With a growl, he yanked her onto his lap so she was straddling him.

He took her mouth, and swallowed her moan. Her tongue tangled with his. One of her hands sank into his hair, tugging hard. She squirmed against him, rocking her damp, bare pussy against the bulge of his cock.

Mav growled.

She bit his lip and he shoved the robe off her.

Now it was just Remi. *Gorgeous.*

He palmed her breast and she arched. He slid his other hand between her thighs.

"Oh, God, *Mav.*"

"You're drenched. For me. Show me how much you want me, angel?"

"I'm on fire." Another moan, and she was riding his hand.

"You need my cock right here." He thrust two fingers inside her.

"Yes, yes," she chanted. "I need you to fuck me, Mav." Her feverish gaze met his. "Hard."

That word arrowed into him. He was big, and he

always kept that in mind when he got naked with a woman.

But the hunger in her gaze drove him to the edge of his control.

He rose. He wasn't fucking her for the first time in his office chair. Not this time.

She wrapped her arms and legs around him. He cupped the sweet curves of her ass.

"Where are you taking me, big guy?"

"My bed. I'm going to fuck you on my bed."

He'd need more than once to calm all this raging need. He needed to touch, taste, and stroke every inch of her. Stake his claim.

Some distant part of his brain warned him that he didn't claim. Not women. Not ever.

But his cock wasn't listening.

He strode up the stairs and into his bedroom.

Morning sunlight poured into the windows, and he laid her on the bed.

She lifted her arms above her head, which pushed her luscious breasts up. She never looked away—not shy or uncertain.

No, his Remi knew exactly what she wanted.

He pushed her legs apart and leaned over her and kissed her. Hard and hungry. She sucked on his tongue.

He broke free, and kissed the side of her neck, and ran his hands over her breasts, kneading the soft curves.

"So gorgeous, Remi."

Her face was flushed, desire in her eyes.

"Look at you," he murmured.

He stroked a hand between her thighs. "Look at this pretty, pink pussy. So wet. I want to lick it, suck it..."

She moaned.

"Spread wider for me."

She obeyed, and he sank two fingers inside her. Remi cried out. Damn, he liked hearing that need in her voice.

Need for him.

"Hold still. I'm going to lick this perfect pussy until you're even wetter, until you're begging for my cock."

"*Mav.*" She arched up.

He buried his face between her legs. She bucked, and he held her down.

Damn. The taste of her... Fucking heaven.

He kept licking and slid his fingers inside. She bucked again, crying out. He kept thrusting his fingers inside her, firm and deep. Then he moved his mouth and found her swollen clit.

"Mav...*God.*"

"I'm going to make you come so many times you'll lose count, angel."

She writhed, her body shaking as he sucked on her clit.

"Oh, oh."

As she screamed, her body stiffened, and then she let go. He watched the pleasure lash her, and she shook, her pussy clenching on his fingers.

Then she fell back, limp and panting. Her eyelids were heavy.

He sat back, and licked his fingers. The taste of her was addicting. "So good."

Watching him, she ran her tongue along her teeth. "Yes."

Mav stood and unbuttoned his shirt. She stayed sprawled there, disheveled, but her gaze was glued to him.

He tore his shirt off, heard her moan. He opened his jeans and shoved them down.

Her eyes widened, and she pushed up on one elbow. "Oh, wow. Big guy was a very appropriate nickname."

"You can take me," he said.

She smiled. "I'll do my best, but you are a lot to take in."

Mav opened the bedside table. She watched him slide the condom on.

He sat on the bed, and lay back on the pillows. She sat up, looking like a pocket-sized goddess.

He grabbed her and yanked her on top of him. "Going to fuck you now, angel."

"Or maybe I'll fuck you."

Sassy as ever. He tugged her closer, her wetness sliding over his abs.

"Ready?" he asked.

She nodded.

"Show me how much you want my cock."

She gripped him. *Fuck.* He almost blew right then and there.

She lifted her hips, guiding him into place. Mav tried to hold on to some sliver of control.

"Take me," he growled. "Take what I need to give you."

She slid down, taking several inches inside her.

As she moaned, he clamped his hands on her ass.

"Mav, you're so big." She sucked in a breath. "Really big."

Their gazes locked. "Take it, angel."

She pressed her hands to his chest. Then she shoved her hips down.

His groan mixed with her sharp cry. Pleasure shot up his spine.

"*Move.*" His voice was a rugged growl. His hands cupped her ass.

Then Remi lifted her hips and started riding him.

Remi

"That's it, angel. Ride me."

God. Mav's sexy growl shivered through me.

I was breathing hard as I worked my hips up and down, riding him hard. I bent forward, hands digging into his firm pecs.

That big cock filled me up. *Mmm.*

I was so full and it felt so good. Every now and then, he'd hit me deep, tearing a moan out of me.

This. *Him.* I needed it. I craved it.

"Fuck." His big hands clamped on my ass, helping me move. Then one of those hands slid up, caught in my hair and clenched.

I could feel my orgasm building, pleasure swelling, huge and a little scary.

Sex wasn't usually this rough or wild. This *much.*

"Harder, angel."

Suddenly, he reared up. He flipped me onto my back, and then that big body was covering me.

He was way bigger, harder, and heavier, but all that did was make me feel safer and more turned on.

"*Mav.*"

"I'm here." He slammed back into me.

With a cry, I arched up and wrapped my legs around his hips.

He hammered into me, that big, thick cock driving hard.

"Oh, God." It was too much, but I still wanted more, not less.

I felt a tremor ripple through his body. Blindly, I stared at him, his rugged face. He kissed me, his lips taking mine, his tongue plunging deep.

He kissed me like I was everything. Like I was his.

Then he ripped free. "Shit, you're tight. You're clutching my cock hard, angel."

I stared at him, the tendons in his neck were strained, his brow creased. He was fucking me hard, but I realized he was holding back a little.

"Mav." I wanted him lost like me. "I..."

Blazing, brown eyes met mine.

"What is it, angel? What do you need?"

"You. All of you."

He frowned, even as he kept thrusting into me.

"Harder," I whispered. "Hold me...down."

Something wild flared in his eyes. "*Remi.*"

I'd never felt safe enough to ask for this before. "I'm sure. Do it."

I already had one hand above my head. The other was clenched on his bicep.

He kept one palm planted on the bed, taking most of his weight. He gripped my hand and slammed it on the bed beside the other.

He took both my wrists with one of his and pressed them into the bed.

Testing him, I pushed against his hold. He didn't budge.

His body tensed, the muscles in his jaw tight. His eyes glittered with a breath-stealing intensity. "Tell me to stop if I get too rough."

I nodded.

His gaze roamed my face. "You mine, angel? Mine to kiss, to stroke? Mine to pin down and fuck until you scream?"

"Yes," I moaned.

He shifted, and slammed back inside me.

I screamed. White-hot pleasure filling me. "Mav—"

"Hold on, angel." His thrusts turned fierce. My body jolted under his.

"I'm going to come," I panted.

"Hold on," he ordered.

I pushed against his big body, bucking. I felt my pussy squeezing his cock. He muttered a raw curse and kept me pinned.

He leaned over me—big, hot, mine. "Come, angel."

I screamed. Pleasure was a flood, and I saw stars. I squeezed him with my legs, and he was my only anchor.

"You're fucking beautiful when you come, Remi."

With a growl, he thrust deeper, then his body stiffened. I watched the pleasure hit him. Then he dropped on me, shuddering.

He was beautiful. Rough, real, and so damn male.

His grip on my wrists eased. He skimmed his hands up my arms and lifted his head.

"Hell, Remi." His breathing was still fast and harsh.

I licked my lips, still trying to catch my breath. "Wow."

"Was I too rough?"

"No." I smacked a kiss to his mouth. "Did you miss the bit where I was begging you to go harder?"

His lips quirked. "Don't move. I've got to deal with this condom."

He pulled out of me and I gave a throaty moan. "Big guy, I'm going to feel you for days."

His eyes flashed. Oh, he liked hearing that.

He strode to the bathroom and I finally got to see that firm ass in all its glory.

I sighed with pleasure.

He glanced back and raised a dark brow.

"You have a superb ass," I told him.

"Thanks."

"And an awesome big cock."

He barked out a laugh.

"Great bod, rugged face, sexy brain."

"You really like my brain?"

I nodded.

He stared at me for a beat, looking a tad confused, then slipped into the bathroom.

I flopped back on the bed. Hmm, I was pretty sure

this decision to bang Mav's brains out would come back to bite me.

But for now, we were working together, and I'd enjoy the hell out of it.

I rolled onto my belly to look at the clock on the bedside table. It was still early. We should monitor the tracker and see what Rayner was up to...

I heard a rough, strangled sound behind me.

I glanced back and saw Mav at the side of the bed, a strange, possessive look on his face.

"What?" I breathed.

"Your back." He grabbed my ankle and pulled me to the edge of the bed, pinning me on my belly.

"Mav!"

A second later, he straddled the backs of my thighs. I felt his hand stroke up my spine and over my shoulder blades. Almost reverent.

"You like my ink," I whispered.

He didn't respond, just kept stroking.

I had a set of intricate angel wings tattooed on my upper back.

He leaned down, and I felt his lips on my skin. I shuddered, already wet between my thighs again.

He pushed forward, that generous cock sliding against my ass cheeks. He was as hard as steel again.

"Mav—"

"On your hands and knees, angel." He jerked my hips up and pressed a palm to the tattoo, then he was inside me.

My head flew back. I gave a garbled cry. So good. Hot, hard, and wet.

He thrust twice, and that's when I realized.

"Mav...condom."

He cursed and pulled out.

"Stay there, Remi. Don't move."

I heard the crinkle of a wrapper. Anticipation screamed through me. Then his hands were back on my shoulder blades.

"Angel. *My* angel. Take me now."

"Yes." I pushed back against him.

Then he filled me.

He moved—not fast, not slow, but firm and deep.

"*Mav.*"

He covered me. "My angel."

"Don't stop. Never stop."

He growled, his hips moving faster. I felt his hands slide under me, and pinch my clit.

I cried out and started coming.

His thrusts got wilder, more out of control. He snarled.

"Fuck, *Remi.*"

Then he was coming inside me, both of us lost in the pleasure.

13

CARAMEL MACCHIATO

Mav

"I'm going to move into your shower."

Mav looked up from the roast beef sandwiches he was making. Remi bounced into the kitchen like she'd never run out of energy.

They'd spent most of the morning in bed, and despite that and a hellish night, here she was, freshly showered and looking bright and bubbly.

She was dressed in leggings that hugged her curves—curves that he was now intimately acquainted with. He knew exactly how her ass felt in his hands as she worked herself on his cock.

Then she'd dozed for a while, half on top of him.

Mav didn't sleep with women. Didn't like to share his bed after sex was done. Hell, he'd never had a woman here at his home—he met them at a hotel, or their place.

He liked Remi on him, her face buried against his

neck as she'd slept. He liked her sleeping on him, worn out from taking him.

"Mav?" She snapped her fingers. She was holding her laptop in her other hand. "Did all that sex fry your brain cells?"

"No."

She jumped up to sit on the island. "I don't know, you're looking kind of dazed." She pressed a hand to his forehead and winked.

She was teasing him.

He liked that, too.

"If you move into my shower, I'll have to charge you rent," he said.

She poked her tongue out. "What's for lunch?"

"Roast beef sandwiches."

Her eyes lit up. "With mustard?"

"Of course."

"Gimme." She held her hand out. "I'm starving."

"I'm not surprised." Because he wanted to, and couldn't stop himself, he stepped closer and kissed her.

She hummed into his mouth, her hand clenching in his hair as she kissed him back.

"Mmm, you taste good, too. Probably almost as good as this roast beef sandwich with mustard."

"Probably?"

She tugged him closer and kissed him again. "Okay, maybe a little better."

He tweaked her ear and passed her the sandwich.

She bit into the food with a small moan, and opened her laptop. He saw that she had the tracking program open. There was a red dot on the Upper East Side.

"Come on, asshole," she said. "Contact The Shadow."

"It's the weekend. He's likely still in bed."

She grunted. "Lazy rich dude."

Mav stood between her legs, hands pressed either side of her hips on the counter. "I'm rich. Do you think I'm lazy?"

She cupped his jaw, her nails scratching over his stubble. "Well, you haven't been this morning."

He kissed her, enjoying her hum of pleasure. Then she pushed him away.

"I have a sandwich to eat. Don't interrupt me."

They ended up eating their lunch on his terrace. He put the outdoor fireplace on and found her a blanket. Watching her curled up on the outdoor couch, munching on her sandwich, and staring at the fire, set off a strange sense of contentment in him.

A few times, Mav pulled out his phone to check the tracker. Whenever she glanced at him, hope in her eyes, he shook his head.

"I'm going to call Mama." Remi rose. "Find out if they've settled in okay."

"Boone will call if there's trouble."

"I know. But this is more for me." She ran her hand down his arm, an easy touch, then slipped inside.

It amazed him that a woman who'd had such a rough start to life was so easy with affection. No doubt another thing Mama Alma was responsible for.

Mav gathered up the plates and headed back inside. From the kitchen, he heard the murmur of her voice from the Great Room, followed by a laugh.

He'd just put the plates in the dishwasher when she returned. She leaned against the island, watching him steadily.

"What?"

"It seems six laptops and a RivSeriesOne gaming system were delivered to the safe house. The boys are currently in fits of delight, trouncing each other in whatever game is their favorite this week. Naomi is starting a cooking blog. Steve is teaching Kaylee how to use her laptop, which you'll be happy to hear she's already covered in stickers. And Mama is resting in bed, watching Netflix on her new machine."

"So, they're good?"

"Mav, you sent thousands of dollars' worth of electronics to them!"

"I wanted them to be comfortable."

She pushed away from the island, grabbed the front of his shirt, and went up on her toes to kiss him. "I like getting a glimpse of the good guy under the gruff."

He scowled. "I'm not a good guy."

She grinned. "Too late. I've seen him. I know he's there."

He growled. "Quit it. Or I'll make you pay."

With a grin, she danced backward. "Ooh, I'm trembling. How are you going to do that, big guy?"

Mav took a step forward. "By spanking that curvy ass of yours."

She gasped, but he didn't miss the way her eyes flared.

His lips curled. "You like the idea of that, angel?"

"You can't spank me...unless you catch me first." She spun and darted around the island.

Desire was a hard, hot punch through his system. He started around the island.

With a laugh, she ran out of the kitchen.

Mav chased her.

They raced through the Great Room, and she dodged behind the couch. She was surprisingly quick.

They ran down the hall, her excited laugh filling the air. She sprinted around the formal dining table and Mav lunged.

He almost caught her, but she yanked free. She raced back toward the Great Room.

"That ass is mine, Solano," he growled.

She tossed him a hot look over her shoulder.

Back in the Great Room, he put on a burst of speed. He snatched her off her feet, loving her laughing yelp. He landed on the couch with Remi on his lap.

He quickly spun her so she was lying facedown, draped over him.

"Mav!" She was breathless and laughing.

He shoved her shirt up, just high enough to see her angel wings. He took a second to trace them, then pulled her leggings and panties down.

She squirmed, and he drank in that gorgeous bare ass. He slapped one smooth cheek.

She gasped.

"God, I love your ass, Remi."

Writhing on him, she lifted a little. He caressed her ass, watching goose bumps rise on her skin. He dipped his hand between her thighs. She was wet.

Mav spanked her again, and again. He turned each slap into a caress, soothing the sting. Soon she was making incoherent cries, lifting her ass up to each slap on her oversensitive skin. He slipped his fingers down to her swollen clit, then sank a finger inside her. She was panting.

"Mav, I won't last much longer."

He rose and laid her flat on the couch. It took him seconds to strip her leggings off. He yanked a condom from his pocket, opened his jeans, and slid the latex on.

"You carry a condom around?" she asked tartly.

"With you here, I do." He covered her body with his, loving the way she wrapped herself around him.

He entered her with a single, deep thrust. They both groaned, her arms flexing on him.

"Perfect," she whispered.

His gaze locked with hers and he started thrusting. This time, he kept his strokes slow and firm, making sure she felt his possession.

"Remi."

"Don't stop."

As he picked up speed a little, driven by a desire he could no longer control, he watched her head drop back. She cried out, her nails digging into his skin.

"I..." Whatever she was going to say was lost as she cried out again. He felt her orgasm take her, felt it in the tight squeeze of her body, saw it on her face.

He pulled her closer, lost in her, and he pounded deeper. His climax hit, hard and powerful. With a deep groan, he dropped his face to her neck and shuddered through his release.

Feeling breathless and out of energy, he dropped to the couch, trying to keep as much weight off her as he could.

She let out a gusty, satisfied sigh.

Mav smiled.

Then she slapped his ass. "Okay, big guy, shake off that post-orgasmic haze. Sexy times, as awesome as they were, are over. We need to find our bad guy."

Mav grunted. "How are you going to get up if I'm lying on top of you?"

She shoved at him, then tried to buck him off, then huffed. "Ugh, you weigh a ton."

"You're just small."

She smacked a kiss to his cheek. "We do need to move."

"I know." He heaved himself up. As much as he wished he could keep Remi locked in his penthouse, preferably in his bed, safe, he knew they had a job to do.

The Calix Project wouldn't be safe, nor would Remi and her family, until they dealt with The Shadow.

Remi

After ducking into Mav's bedroom to clean up, I headed back downstairs to meet him in his office.

My body still felt warm, loose, and luscious. Who knew spanking could be so much fun? Or wild, sexy couch sex?

Don't get too used to it, Remi.

And I couldn't afford to let myself get distracted from the asshole threatening my family. My gut churned.

Mav was already at his computer. My laptop was set up beside him.

I dropped into the chair and studied the tracker screen. *Nothing*.

"Come on," I cried. "Rayner can't still be in bed."

"I did a little searching."

A photo from a nightclub popped up. It showed a very drunk-looking Leon with his trio of buddies from Guastavino's. There were a few women with them.

"Rayner had a very late night."

I huffed out a frustrated breath. "Waiting sucks."

"It does."

A notification popped up on his screen and I looked at it. "Someone called Martine needs you to approve the donation increase for the Kids Tech Fund."

Mav grunted, opened an email and started typing.

Frowning, I opened a browser and typed in Kids Tech Fund.

A large charity that donated tech—computers, software, electronics—to schools and holiday programs. It focused mainly on inner city schools, but it helped schools all across the country. I sucked in a breath. It was funded by private donors. I suspected one donor in particular.

"Kids Tech Fund, huh?" I said.

Mav glanced my way.

"Funded by private donors."

He grunted. "I make a lot of tax-deductible donations."

"Including some pretty hefty ones to help disadvantaged kids learn to use tech, learn to code, to gain the skills they'll need in today's workplace?"

Mav stared at his computer screen so hard I was surprised I didn't see holes bored into it.

Feeling warm and gooey inside, I leaned over and kissed his stubbled cheek. "There's that good guy again."

He flicked me a glance. "Do you want another spanking?"

I felt a sweet little pulse in my lower belly. "Yes, but not right now." I shifted in my chair. "My ass cheeks are a little sensitive."

Heat ignited in his eyes.

"And there is something I *really* need."

"What? I'll give it to you."

I cocked my head. "I need a triple, venti, half sweet, non-fat caramel macchiato from Starbucks."

He eyed me like I'd lost my mind. "A what?"

"A big caramel macchiato with—"

He held up a hand. "I don't want to know."

"I know you drink your coffee black, but when I'm stressed, I really need my fix from Starbucks."

Mav sighed. "It isn't safe to go out. If The Shadow is watching my place—"

"We'll put on ballcaps and sneak out the back. Just to Starbucks and back. Please? This waiting is killing me."

He rubbed the back of his neck. "Fine."

"Yay." I jumped up and kissed him again. "I'll get my shoes. Wait. Where are my shoes?"

"They were covered in soot. They're in the laundry room."

"Oh my God, I didn't bring extra shoes."

He shook his head. "I'll grab them and get some hats."

My running shoes were pretty grimy but I cleaned them off the best I could. Mav gave me a New York Giants ballcap and I stuffed my hair under it. His hat was a New York Rangers one.

"Hey, I like ice hockey more than football," I said.

"Me too." The hat did little to hide his rugged face. He pulled on a tan suede jacket and I slipped into my own puffy, blue coat.

We headed down in the elevator.

"There's a Starbucks a couple of blocks away." Once we got outside, he took my hand.

And I found myself braving the cold day, walking down a pretty SoHo street, holding hands with a billionaire.

Funny, I didn't really think about the billionaire thing so much now. He was just Mav.

When we stepped inside the Starbucks, I absorbed the warm air. It wasn't too busy.

"You want something?" I asked Mav.

"Hell, no." He scanned around the place, eyeing the few people inside, including the baristas.

I leaned into him. "I don't think any of the baristas are out to kill us."

He shot me a look.

I placed my order and made my way to the end of the counter to wait. Mav stood beside me, shoulders hunched.

As we waited, I wondered what Mama and the kids were doing.

"Remi?" a voice said.

My head jerked up and I saw a slim man in ironed jeans and a black hoodie. His hoodie had the words "I'd rather be phishing" written on the front. His light brown hair was neatly combed, his skin was pale white, and he fidgeted a little.

"I'm *so* glad I found you."

His voice registered. "Wesley?"

He smiled at me.

"God, how did you find me here?" I asked.

"I traced your phone. You haven't been answering my messages."

He'd what? *Oh, my God.*

Mav stepped closer to me, his hand dropping to my shoulder. "Remi, who the hell is this?"

I sucked in a breath.

Wesley straightened. "I'm her boyfriend."

I felt Mav stiffen. I looked up and my stomach clenched to a tiny point. As I watched, his face hardened, his eyes going blank. His hand dropped away from me.

For a second, I knew he was seeing Hannah.

You idiot, Mav. I faced Wesley. "Wesley, you aren't my boyfriend. Never have been and never will be. I told you I only wanted to be friends, and I tried to be nice and not hurt you."

"We're hackers, Remi," he said insistently. "We have the same work and hobbies. We're a good match."

"No, we're not. You don't even know me. This is the first time we've met in real life." I glanced at Mav and saw several things working in his gaze now. "And Wes, tracing me via my phone, that's creepy."

Wesley's face fell. "I...I don't want to be creepy."

I tried to remind myself he was just a lonely guy, with limited social skills.

Wesley swallowed. "Is there someone else?"

I sighed. "Yes."

His gaze moved past me to Mav. "Him?"

"Yes, not that it's any of your business."

Wesley straightened to his full height, which still put him several inches shorter than Mav. "She's an amazing woman. You couldn't treat her right."

I swallowed a groan.

"Caramel macchiato for Angel?" the barista called out.

"That's me." I grabbed the coffee and turned back.

Wesley was trying to stare down Mav, who now looked vaguely amused.

"Wes, go home."

"No, I want to know who this guy is? He could be a criminal. He could be using you."

I choked and heard Mav's low chuckle.

Wesley glared at Mav. "I think we should take this outside."

Oh my God, what did my sort-of hacker friend think he was going to do with Mav? Fight him? Mav would take him down with one punch.

"Wesley, no—"

"Remi?" a deep voice said from behind me.

I spun and saw Killian. My boss wasn't in his suit today, but he was still wearing black. Black jeans and a black turtleneck that fit his lean, muscular form, topped with a black leather jacket.

I blinked. "Killian, how did you find me?"

"I traced your phone."

I huffed out a breath. I had extra security on my phone. How the hell was everyone hacking into it today?

Wesley was goggling at Killian. My boss looked sharp, sexy, and dangerous in a kind of badass assassin way.

Killian meanwhile was looking at Mav. "Rivera."

"Hawke," Mav replied.

"Wait," Wesley breathed. "Rivera?" He studied Mav's face hard under the brim of the cap. His mouth dropped open. "Maverick Rivera. Oh wow, Remi. You're sleeping with Maverick Rivera!"

"What the fuck?" Killian bit out. "What the hell have you dragged Remi into, Rivera?" His dark gaze locked on my face. "I found out about the fire. Are you okay?"

"So much for our disguises," Mav grumbled.

"Killian," I said. "I'm fine."

"Wait," Wesley said. "Killian Hawke from Sentinel Security." Wes breathed my boss' name like he was a rockstar. He glanced at me. "Are you sleeping with him too?"

My patience, which wasn't that great to begin with, snapped. "Okay, Wesley, it is none of your business who I sleep with. And don't ever track my phone again, or I will hack your computer and make you regret it. Understand?"

His shoulders slumped and he nodded.

"Killian, I'm fine. Mav didn't get me into this mess, I did. He's helping me."

Killian reached for my arm. "You're mine, Remi. You should have contacted me."

Mav pushed up behind me, his big chest pressing against my back. "She isn't yours."

"Cool it, Rivera, I mean she works for me, so that makes her one of mine. I look after my people."

Mav slid an arm around me. "Well, she's in my bed, so that makes her well and truly mine."

I cocked a hip. "Why don't you just brand me? That should limit the confusion." I tried to pull away but Mav held me tight. I released a breath. "I actually belong to myself, but Mav is helping me, and I promise things will be fine. Eventually."

Killian stared at my face, then reluctantly nodded. He skewered Mav with a laser stare. "You'd better take good care of her or I will make you pay."

Mav just grunted.

Jeez, the alpha male displays were half annoying, half sexy.

Then something finally clicked in my head. "Wait. How did you two trace my phone? I have it locked down."

Killian frowned. "I got a tracking message from you, telling me where you were."

Wesley nodded. "I did too."

My blood turned to ice. "I didn't send any messages."

Behind me, Mav stiffened. "The Shadow got into your phone."

"And sent a tracking message out. Probably to *all* my recently used contacts, knowing that bogus email address of his was there too." My pulse pounded. "He knows where I am."

Mav snatched my phone, dropped it to the floor, then stomped his boot on it.

It crunched to tiny pieces.

Killian crossed his arms over his chest. "I think you'd better share exactly what the hell is going on."

I tasted bile. I didn't want Killian in danger as well. "No, I—"

Suddenly, the front windows of the Starbucks shattered in a hail of gunfire.

14

I JUST NEED YOU

Mav

Mav leaped on Remi, pinning her to the floor.
"Everyone, get down!" he roared.

Beside him, Killian yanked Wesley down, shoving the young hacker behind an armchair.

More gunfire hit and more glass broke. He heard bullets thud into something nearby. Beneath him, he felt Remi shaking.

"We need to crawl away from the windows," he said against her ear.

She nodded.

He lifted his weight off her, keeping his body between her and the window. They crawled across the floor, through her spilled coffee, toward the back of the coffeeshop. He saw other customers huddled under tables. Thankfully, no one appeared to be hurt.

Stopping, he yanked Remi close, keeping himself wrapped around her.

Closer to the windows, Killian rose cautiously. He had a black handgun clutched in his hand. He moved toward the door, peering out through the glass.

He glanced at Mav with a silent warning to stay, then slipped outside.

"God, is it over?" Remi whimpered.

"Just hold tight, angel. I've got you."

She clung to him.

Killian was back a moment later, his gun no longer in view. "Shooter's gone."

"Thank God," a customer cried out.

"I'm calling 9-1-1," a barista shouted. "Everyone sit tight."

Fuck. Mav didn't want to stay here. He wanted Remi back at his place, safe.

Nearby, Wesley was sitting up, rocking a little. He looked shell shocked.

"Jesus, Mav," Remi said. "The Shadow could have killed all these people—" her voice hitched "—just to get to me."

He stroked a hand down her back. "It's all right. No one was hurt."

Killian knelt and handed out a key fob. "My ride's out front. Gray Range Rover. It's armored. Get her somewhere safe."

Mav took the keys. "Thanks, Hawke. I owe you."

"Just keep her safe." Killian looked at Remi. "If you need me, call."

"Thanks, Kill," she murmured.

"Come on." Mav helped her up. He hustled her

outside, and as they headed for the Range Rover, it unlocked automatically.

As fast as he could, he got Remi in the passenger seat. Once he slid behind the steering wheel, he started the SUV and pulled out. The wheels screeched, and he forced himself to relax, hands flexing on the wheel.

Fucking hell. He blew out a long breath. He took the long way back to his place and once they were in his garage, he carefully scanned around.

He wasted no time getting Remi into the elevator and upstairs. Inside his place, he checked his security system, and made sure it was engaged.

Then he turned. His heart clenched.

Remi had her arms around herself, her shoulders hunched. Her caramel macchiato had ended up spilled down the front of her.

He cupped her chin and saw misery in her eyes.

"It's never going to end. He'll keep coming until he kills me, or you, or my family." She bit her lip and shook her head. "I couldn't live if you or Mama, or the kids—"

"Hey." He yanked her to his chest, holding her tight. He was clearly getting the hang of the hugging thing, as this didn't feel odd at all.

She gripped onto him and he felt dampness on his shirt. Looking down, he saw the tears tracking down her cheeks and felt a moment of panic.

"Don't cry."

She sniffled. "I can't exactly control it, Mav."

"Try." He rubbed a soothing hand up and down her back. "I promise you, we will find this asshole, and we will stop him."

She looked up at him. The tears were slowing. "Together."

"Together. Maverick Rivera and his Rogue Angel."

That got him a twitch of her lips.

"Why don't I run you a bath? You can soak in there and relax."

She tilted her head. "Have you ever run a bath before?"

"No." He'd never used the tub in the master bathroom. "How hard can it be? Dump in some smelly stuff and run the water."

"There's that nice Maverick guy again."

"I can put you in the bath with a red ass."

She giggled. "A bath sounds nice."

"Good." In the bathroom, he turned on the water in the marble tub, and found a bottle of something lavender smelling in the cabinet under one of the sinks. He dumped some in and bubbles frothed.

When he turned, he found a now-naked Remi standing in the bathroom.

His cock twitched.

Shit, they'd been shot at. She was scared, upset, probably still in a bit of shock. He got a lock on his desire.

"Get in the tub." Crap, his voice held a rough edge.

Remi didn't seem to mind. She just smiled, stroked his arm, and slipped into the tub. She leaned back, closed her eyes, and let out a little sigh.

Good. He let himself stroke her cheekbone. "I'll be in my office. Just yell if you need anything."

"Thanks, Mav."

He slipped out before he stripped off his clothes and got in with her.

In his office, he checked the tracker—still nothing—and answered a few emails. He flicked through a report that Richard was waiting on. His CFO got testy if reports were late.

Well over an hour had passed when he heard a noise in the doorway. He felt a little flash of déjà vu seeing Remi standing there, bundled up in a robe. He held out a hand to her.

She reached for it, fingers curling around his. She perched on the arm of his chair. "Rayner?"

"Nothing."

She nodded. "It's a little early, but will you come to bed. I don't want to sleep without you."

He pressed his forehead to hers. "Whatever you need, angel."

"I just need you," she whispered.

Mav

The next morning, Mav stood in his kitchen, making coffee for himself and Remi.

He sipped his black one, then stirred more creamer into hers. She and Liam would probably bond over sweet, milky coffee.

Mav's gut tightened. He realized he wanted to introduce her to his friends. Wanted them to like each other.

Yesterday, at Starbucks, he'd had a moment where

he'd thought for a second that Remi was another Hannah. Wesley had stood there, proclaiming to be her boyfriend, and Mav had been plunged back to college and the entire mess with Hannah.

But he realized it had just been a split-second gut reaction. He *knew* Remi. He knew she was fiercely loyal to those she loved. Knew she'd never betray someone who was hers.

He'd known her a week. He shook his head. He shouldn't be so ready to trust her.

"Okay, I've changed my mind, I'm moving into your bathtub."

Remi skipped into the kitchen, holding the new Riv 6+ phone he'd given her to replace her destroyed one. She was in a pair of black leggings, with a silky-looking, white sweater and a denim jacket over the top. Her hair was out today and sometime since he'd left her well-pleasured in his bed this morning, she'd painted her nails. They were now red and black, painted diagonally across the nail.

She looked refreshed. There was no sign of the dejection and fear from the night before. She'd just bounced back. Mav pressed his lips together. He'd like to make it so she didn't have to roll with the punches.

"I'll still charge you rent."

Smiling, she walked up to him, sliding her hands up his chest. "I think I could get around you."

"I'm no pushover, Solano." He looked at her hands. "I like your nails."

"This is my 'hunting the bad guy' look."

He didn't want her thinking about The Shadow just yet and tugged her closer.

"Wait," she said. "Rayner—"

"Nothing yet." Mav kissed her, sliding his hands around to cup her ass.

With a tiny moan, she kissed him back. He lifted her onto the island, shoving her legs apart.

Things were just getting interesting, when his phone rang.

He groaned. "I have to get that."

"Really?" She shimmied against him.

"It's my mom."

"What?" She let go of him at lightning speed.

Smiling, he grabbed his phone. "Hi, Mom."

"*Buenos dias, mi hijo.* I hope you're relaxing."

"I am."

Remi tried to wriggle away from him, but he held her tight.

"How are you, Mom?"

"Good, good. Your father and I are in the city today. We're just around the corner from your place. Are you free for coffee with your parents?"

Oh, hell. Mav glanced at Remi. "Sure, Mom."

"Wonderful. See you in a few minutes."

"See you soon."

Remi impersonated a statue. "See you soon?"

"My parents are about to drop in for a quick visit."

Her eyes went as wide as dinner plates. "What?" Her voice was a squeak.

"My parents—"

"I heard you." She leaped off the island. "I'll hide in your office."

"You are not hiding." He scowled at her.

"What are you going to tell them?"

"That you're a friend." He hadn't put labels on what was going on with Remi, but he wasn't hiding her. He could lie to himself, but not to his parents.

"A friend? Just hanging around barefoot at your place on a Sunday?" She made a sound, then raced around. "Where are my shoes?"

He grabbed her upper arms. "It's fine. Calm down. We'll say you're here working on a special project."

She sucked in a breath. "Okay. That should work."

She disappeared out of the kitchen and Mav rinsed out his coffee mug.

When he looked up, she had her laptop at the kitchen table, and a pair of dark-framed glasses perched on her nose.

He stilled. "Where did those come from?"

She looked up. "What?"

Desire was like a punch to his stomach. "The glasses?"

"Oh, my laptop bag. They don't have a prescription. I find if I wear them at cafés when I'm on my laptop, people leave me alone to work. Glasses have power. Ask Clark Kent."

He wouldn't leave her to do anything. He strolled over and caught her chin. "Later, I want you in my bed, wearing those glasses and nothing else."

Her lips twitched, and her gaze dropped to the hardening bulge in his jeans. "You have a glasses fetish, Rivera?"

"No, I've got a Remi-in-glasses fetish."

The doorbell rang and her smile vanished.

"It's going to be fine," he said.

Mav walked to the front door and let his parents in.

"Mom."

His mother hugged him, then cocked her head. "You look good."

"Thanks. You too." He kissed her cheek. "Hi, Dad."

"Mav." His father hugged him and they slapped backs.

"We met some friends for brunch," his mother said.

"Late breakfast," his father grumbled. "It doesn't need a fancy name."

"We have a surprise for you," his mother continued. "We—"

As they walked into the kitchen, his mother's gaze snagged on Remi, who was doing her best to look professional.

"Who's this?" his mother breathed.

"Mom, Dad, this is Remi."

"Hello," Remi said with a nod.

Mav waved her over and she glared. He realized this was about the barefoot thing. He jerked his head and she came reluctantly.

"I'm Remi. I'm working with Mr. Rivera on a project."

"Really?" his mother said. "On a Sunday?"

"An *urgent* project," Remi said.

His mother looked at Mav. She was well aware that

he didn't let many people into his private domain, but Remi didn't know that.

"You might not be aware, but your son is a workaholic," Remi said.

"Oh, we know," his mother said.

"And a bit bossy."

His mom's lips quirked. "I know that, too."

His mother looked extremely happy. The door buzzed again.

"Oh, that's your surprise." She hustled out toward the front door. "Look who we found downstairs."

As Zane and Liam strolled in, Mav ground his teeth together. *Oh, crap.* They saw Remi and froze. Remi looked like she'd stopped breathing.

"What is *she* doing here?" Zane asked.

"They're working on a project," Mav's mom said.

"I bet they are," Liam murmured.

"Ah..." Remi took a step toward the door. "I need to check something in the office." Then she fled.

Remi

I escaped into Mav's home office.

God. His place was now full of people. The office door flung open and I spun.

Zane Roth stormed in, followed by Liam Kensington.

I lifted my chin.

"You're a hacker and a traitor," Zane said. "You're blackmailing Mav and we won't let you hurt him."

"You don't understand," I said.

Zane shook his head. "I know a woman stomped on his trust once. I know you've ensnared him—"

I laughed. "You think I somehow got him obsessed with me?" I waved a hand. "Me? Yes, I'm a regular femme fatale. You have no idea what's going on here."

"Really?" Liam picked up my discarded robe off the floor.

Heat flooded my cheeks. "Look, Mav and I are working together. He doesn't want to drag you both into it. He knows you've been through your own crap lately."

They both stared at her, frowning.

The door opened again.

Mav blocked the doorway, and scowled at his friends and strode straight to me. He wrapped an arm around me.

So much for pretending things were purely professional.

"Where are your parents?" I asked.

"Making coffee." He looked at his friends. "Remi is a white-hat hacker who works for Sentinel Security."

"Killian Hawke's company," Liam said.

"Yes. Her foster mother is sick, and a not-so-friendly someone bribed her into hacking my system."

"They wouldn't take no for an answer," I said quietly.

Mav squeezed my shoulders. "They set her family home on fire, and chained the doors closed. With her foster mother and siblings inside."

Zane muttered a curse. Liam's face was suffused with anger.

Zane's gaze met mine. "Are they all right?"

I nodded.

"Boone got them out," Mav added. "I hired him to watch them. Then yesterday, we were shot at while we were at Starbucks."

Liam sucked in a breath. "I heard about that shooting. Are you both all right?"

"We're fine," Mav said.

"You should have called." Zane stepped closer and dragged a hand through his dark hair. "I'm sorry." He looked directly at me. "I'm sorry I was hard on you. We were just worried about him."

I swallowed. "He has good friends. I don't want him hurt, either."

"Remi and I are going to find The Shadow. Unmask him."

Zane cursed.

"This is a dangerous game," Liam said.

"He's after military secrets," Mav growled. "And he's willing to kill innocent people, kids. I won't let that stand."

Mav's friends didn't look happy but they nodded.

"What can we do to help?" Zane asked.

"Nothing."

"Mav—"

He held up a hand. "I don't have anything yet, but we're working on it. If we need help, I'll call."

"Promise?" Liam looked at me. "He's notorious for trying to do everything himself, and not asking for help."

I smiled. "Noted."

"I promise," Mav said with the grumpy growl. "I already gave Vander a heads up."

Remi cocked her head. "Who's Vander?"

"Vander Norcross. Ex-military. Runs a security company."

Zane nodded. "He's helped us out in the past and does work for Roth Enterprises. Guy is spooky, scary, and gets the job done."

"The boogeyman," Remi said.

"No," Mav said. "He's the guy the boogeyman is afraid of."

The computer on the desk let out an insistent chime.

Still scowling, Mav leaned over it.

"What is it?" I asked.

"Rayner made some calls and sent some messages."

My heart leaped. "Is the dragon angel working?"

His brows drew together. "Too well." He shifted.

On-screen was the map of the United States. A red tangle of lines was spreading out like an infection from New York.

I frowned. "No, it's tracking *everyone* in his network."

"And everyone connected to them."

"Can we limit it? Find a way to narrow it to The Shadow?"

A muscle ticked in his jaw. "Not easily. We need more computer power."

I watched the map turning red.

We need a lot more power. *Dammit.*

"God, they're perfect for each other," Zane murmured.

"There must be something we can do," I said ignoring the billionaire. "I'm *not* letting that asshole win. I let Rayner pinch my ass to get that trojan on his phone."

Mav's face turned to stone. "He what?"

"Stay focused, big guy. We need to think."

"No, we need more computer power. Luckily, I have that."

My head whipped up.

"At the Rivera Tech Park upstate."

I gasped. "Oh my God, I've always wanted to see inside of that place."

"Yes, perfect for each other," Liam whispered.

Mav smiled. "Today's your lucky day, angel."

"He's smiling again," Zane said.

"I know," Liam replied. "I'm still not used to it."

"All right, you two need to get back to your women," Mav said. "We need to get to Rivera Tech Park."

"Okay, you guys be careful," Zane said.

After Mav showed his friends out, we tracked down his parents. They were finishing their coffees in the living room.

"I'm sorry, Mom and Dad, Remi and I need to go to my labs at Syracuse. It's important."

His mom gave him a look I'd seen on Mama Alma's face too many times to count, then she nodded. She must've picked up on the seriousness.

Mav hugged his mom. I fought off the edgy itchiness. I wanted to get to work, and away from the scrutiny of Mav's parents.

"To make it up to me, you need to come home for a family dinner next week," Mrs. Rivera said.

"Okay, Mom."

I felt a little flash of heat on my cheeks. Was there

anything sweeter than a big, strong man who clearly adored his mother?

"And bring Remi," Mrs. Rivera continued.

"What?" My eyes widened. I shook my head, but Mav pretended not to notice.

Then Mrs. Rivera turned my way and I smiled.

"I'd love to, Mrs. Rivera, but I—"

She gave me the mom look. Wow, that really packed a punch.

"I'd love to," I said in a rush.

Dammit.

Mrs. Rivera beamed, patted Mav's arm, and then touched my cheek.

Mav's dad just smiled at us.

After they'd left, I decided to ignore the dinner thing. "I'll pack my laptop."

He nodded. "I'll get your shoes."

Soon we were in his sexy, little roadster, zipping down the street. My sooty shoes couldn't be helped. I just hoped I didn't make a mess in his fancy car.

When he drove into a garage at the Rivera Tech head office, I frowned. "Do you need to pick something up from here?"

"Yeah." He grabbed my laptop bag and swung it onto his shoulder.

He used a fingerprint scanner and retinal scan to get us into the building. Soon, we were in an elevator, shooting upward.

In my head, I calculated how long it would take us to drive to Rivera Tech Park. Every hour of delay was time wasted. I wanted The Shadow exposed. I wanted Mama and my family safe.

"Have you heard from Boone?" I asked.

"Yes, he's busy trying to beat Charlie and Jamal at Mario Kart. And Naomi is cooking up enough food for all of Long Island."

The tension inside me eased a little. They were safe.

"I told him to give them your new number," Mav added.

The elevator doors opened and I frowned. This wasn't Mav's office.

"What are we doing?" I asked.

He pushed open an external door. "Getting our ride to the lab."

The whump-whump-whump of rotors hit me. I stepped out and sucked in a breath.

A sleek, black helicopter sat on the helipad, the side door open and the rotors spinning.

The Rivera Tech logo was painted on the side of it.

Mav waved a hand. "After you."

15

_____

RIVERA TECH PARK

Mav

A short while later, the helicopter swept in over
Rivera Tech Park.

Several large, hexagonal-shaped buildings were
surrounded by lush gardens, and not far away were
several enormous warehouses, with assembly lines for
tech they constructed locally. Mav tried to provide as
many local jobs as he could.

Beside him, Remi bounced in her seat, nose pressed
to the side window of the helicopter.

She didn't hide a single ounce of her joy and
curiosity.

The helicopter pulled in, hovered, and then landed
on the helipad outside the main building. Remi caught
his eye and smiled.

"There you go, Mr. Rivera," the pilot called back.

"Thank you, Mark." Mav open the side door, climbed
out, and then helped Remi out.

"Wow," she mouthed.

A man in pressed pants and a checked shirt with a lanyard dangling around his neck strode across the helipad to meet them. Dr. Ruben Jones, a tall, lanky, African-American man in wire-rimmed glasses, was the head of operations.

"Didn't know you'd be visiting on a Sunday afternoon, Mav."

"Chill, Ruben, I'm working on a special project, and needed some more computer power. Ruben, this is Remi. Remi, Ruben's the boss around here."

"Hi." She shook Ruben's hand. "The place looks great." She took in all the glass walls of the building, and the green interior walls visible through the glass. There were plants everywhere.

"You work in tech, Remi?" Ruben asked.

She nodded. "Cybersecurity."

"Well, wait until you get a look at Mav's computer lab."

Remi grinned. "I can't wait."

Mav rolled his eyes. "We don't want to be disturbed while we're in my lab."

"You got it," Ruben replied. "There are only a few people here today, anyway."

They headed down the hall. Ruben showed them the kitchen area near the lab—fully stocked with a coffee machine, sodas, and snacks.

Remi grabbed a cookie. "Must be nice to work here." She took a bite.

"Most people like it," Mav said.

"Unfortunately, there are always a couple who are

unhappy." Ruben glanced at Mav. "You got the report on Tisdale?"

Mav scowled. "Yeah."

"Security caught him trying to cut through the fence on the eastern side of the park a few days ago."

Remi raised a brow.

"Disgruntled employee," Mav said. "He was fired recently."

"He has a mental illness, and he's not taking his meds," Ruben said.

"Tisdale believes my phones are secretly embedding microchips in people's fingers. So I can control the world," Mav said, deadpan.

Remi bit her lip. "You do look like an evil mastermind."

He wanted to kiss her and swat her butt, but he managed to restrain himself.

"You gave him enough chances, Mav," Ruben said. "The lawyers are going to press charges this time."

Mav sighed. "Fine."

They reached a large door that was marked Comp Lab 15.

"If you need anything, let me know. I'll be in my office."

"Thanks, Ruben."

The man nodded his head at Remi. "Nice to meet you, Remi."

"You, too."

Mav pressed a hand to a scanner beside the door and it beeped. The door slid open, and he led her inside.

She gasped. "Oh. My. God."

It was his own little space. He led her past the line of servers to the heart of the lab.

"This is my private lab." He felt a funny sensation. He spent a lot of time here, when he could escape the city and the meetings.

She turned in a circle—taking in the computer screens, the large digital board, the workbenches covered in tools and half-built prototypes.

She met his gaze. "This is *awesome*."

He smiled, chest filled with...something.

"Can I see your system now?" She fluttered her lashes.

"You have to buy me dinner first," he said.

"How about a bite of cookie?" She held up what was left of her cookie.

Mav bit it, purposely letting his tongue touch her fingers.

She bit her lip, watching his mouth.

As he chewed on his mouthful of cookie, he waved at the chair in front of the main screens. "All yours, angel."

She moved fast, and scrambled into the chair. He figured he should be insulted that she was so desperate to test out his computer, almost forgetting about him in the process.

Except, he realized that she was looking at it much the same way she'd looked at his mouth. His gut clenched.

"Nice." She tapped, zooming through his system. Her eyebrows winged up. "When you said more computer power, I didn't expect this!"

Mav sat beside her. "I wanted the best, most powerful system in the world."

"Of course, you did." She cracked her knuckles. "Now, let's get to work."

Mav tapped the keyboard, and pulled up his tracker and all the info.

"One of these dots is The Shadow." She tapped her nails on the desk. "We need to use a few parameters to track him down."

"We can't assume that he's in New York."

She swiveled. "You don't think so?"

"He could be in a foreign nation, or an international terrorist organization."

She shuddered. "I really hope not. Okay, let's see if I can narrow down some dates and times. Maybe link it to that bogus Gmail email account."

Her fingers flew.

Soon, she was absorbed. He really liked watching her work.

The computer pinged. It was an internal Rivera Tech chat window and he opened it. Rollo's face and disheveled hair appeared.

"Mav-man. Didn't know you were coming out here today."

"Hey, Rollo." He waved at Remi to stay out of sight. "I'm working on a special project."

The man's eyebrows winged up. "Need help?"

"No, thanks."

Rollo tossed him a salute. "Just give a shout if you do." The man stuck his hand in a bag of chips. "I'm just down the hall."

The screen went black.

"How's it going?" Mav asked her.

Her brow creased. "It's taking longer than I'd hoped."

He leaned closer. "I have another algorithm I've been working on. It might speed things up."

"Show me."

They worked together. He liked how her brain tackled problems. Mav was more linear and direct in his thinking, but Remi's brain seemed to toss out a bunch of different ideas all at once.

"Okay. Search parameters are in." He hit a key.

"Wow, that algorithm rocks." She smiled at him and pressed a quick kiss to his cheek.

It was just a casual, fleeting kiss, but he felt it to his toes.

"I think you might be a genius, Rivera."

"Time magazine said I was."

She grinned. "Show off."

She flicked the search up on the screen and he saw the progress bar at 3%. It ticked to 4%.

"It's still going to take a while." Her fingernails tapped on the desk.

"But it will be far less than before. You just need a little patience."

"That's one virtue I can't claim." She eyed him, something changing in her gaze. "Do you have any cameras in here?"

He frowned. "No, just outside the door in the hall."

"Good." She rose, and closed the gap between them.

"Why?" he asked slowly.

She dropped to her knees. "Because I thought of something pleasurable we could do to pass the time."

As her hands slid up his thighs, every muscle in Mav's body locked. "Oh?"

She smiled, her fingers moving to his belt buckle.

"Yes, I'm going to suck that big cock of yours."

Remi

I felt the tension vibrating in Mav's big body.

Because of me.

Oh yeah, I loved driving this man wild.

I finished unbuckling his belt and opened his jeans. His thick cock sprang free.

Hot flames licked at my belly. I was almost shaking with the need to touch him, pleasure him. I gripped his cock, and stroked down to the base. He let out a low groan.

"What was that, Mr. Rivera?" she teased.

"I can't think with your face so close to my cock."

"Good." I leaned in. God, he was so thick and long.

"And feeling you breathing on it makes it even worse," he added.

That bossy, grumpy tone got to me every time.

"Clamp those big hands of yours on the arms of your chair. I'm in charge now."

His dark eyes flashed. "Really?"

I pumped his cock and got another groan. "Really."

"I can't believe I'm letting you do this." His voice was a growl.

"Like I said, you aren't in charge."

"Remi, put your mouth on me before I lose my mind."

My gaze locked on his. That hungry expression on his rugged face made me wet between my legs.

Staring at him, I leaned closer and licked the head of his cock. He growled. Oh, that need, that hunger was all for me.

I licked again, swirling my tongue around the swollen head of his erection. My hair slid forward, brushing his skin.

He jerked in the chair, and I saw his knuckles turn white as he gripped the armrests.

I closed my mouth on his cock and sucked.

His tortured groan sent up butterflies in my belly. With a growl, one of his hands slid into my hair, massaging my scalp.

The man just had to take charge. Luckily, I liked it, and because he wasn't directing or forcing me, I just closed my eyes and kept working him.

"You're so damn hot, Remi. You drive me *crazy*."

His voice was so guttural that I could barely understand him.

I swirled my tongue, and heard him suck in a breath. Gently, he nudged me further down, his cock going deep.

My fingers dug into his hard thighs.

"God, angel." He growled. "That's it, swallow me."

I moved up and down—taking him deep, then moving until just the head was in my mouth.

I loved his cock. I loved driving him wild. His big body vibrated under me, his fingers firm against my scalp.

"Angel… *Remi…*"

His hips bucked up, driving him deeper. My vision blurred, sensation exploding. Shit, I was going to come just from this.

He grunted, then groaned my name. With another thrust, he came, exploding down my throat.

I trembled, on the verge of my own climax.

He gently eased out of my mouth, and then I was yanked onto his lap.

I was panting.

"That mouth of yours." He yanked me in and kissed me.

I squirmed, desire leaving me needy and lightheaded.

"What's my angel need?" His brown eyes were on me —hot, and filled with something I couldn't put a name to.

Or maybe I was afraid to, in case I was just imagining what I wanted to see.

His hands slid down my thighs, back up and inside my leggings.

"Mav," I gasped.

"Shh, now I'm going to give you what you need."

His hand went straight into my panties.

"So wet, angel. You love my cock, don't you?"

His knuckles rubbed my clit. On a husky cry, I exploded.

My body jerked and shuddered. Mav held me tight, rubbing my clit until I touched his hand and pushed him away.

His strong arms closed around me.

With a contented sigh, I leaned back against him. Again, I felt that safe feeling.

I closed my eyes. Part of me said not to trust it. People had been disappearing all my life. Letting me down. Hearts were so damn hard to repair, so it was better to keep it light, have fun, and not risk anything deeper.

I kissed the underside of his jaw.

"That was nice," I said.

"Nice?"

"Sorry. That was off-the-charts, mind blowing."

He pinched my side. "That's better."

"Hot sex with you is a definite side benefit of this whole situation."

I saw him frown.

The computer pinged.

"It's Ruben," he said.

I scrambled up and out of view. I needed to tidy up. I grabbed a bottle of water off the desk and sipped.

On the screen, Ruben was frowning. Behind him, I heard an alarm going off.

"Mav," Ruben said. "We have a minor security breach."

"Oh?" Mav said, stiffening.

Ruben sighed. "It's Tisdale." The director shook his head. "He cut the fence. The security team's been dispatched."

"Okay. He really needs help, Ruben."

"I know. We've tried. He's a smart guy, but his demons are hard to tame, and right now he doesn't seem to want to tame them."

Mav nodded, and pressed a hand to the back of his neck. "Keep me posted."

The chat window closed.

"You feel bad for him," I said.

"Of course. Tisdale was a good employee. A good guy. It's upsetting and frustrating to see him like this, and not be able to help him."

I wrapped my arms around Mav and hugged him. "You're a good guy, Maverick Rivera."

An insistent chime came from the computer.

"What now?" Mav's face changed, and my heart did a flip.

"The tracker narrowed down to an address," Mav said. "In Manhattan."

"Oh my God, where?" I leaned over his shoulder.

"In SoHo."

I felt a chill. "That's just around the block from your place."

"A three-story house."

I looked at the image he pulled up. It was a plain rectangular, corner building painted a dark gray, with narrow balconies on all sides. It didn't look like much, but I knew it would be worth millions.

Mav tapped in a search. "Fuck. It's a rental."

"Rented by…?"

"Zaria Corp." He tapped again. "I can't find anything on them."

"Let me." My fingers danced. "It's a shell company." I groaned. "A real tangle of shell companies."

"Dammit," Mav bit out.

"Hang on." I opened up a chat window, and a second later, Killian's handsome face appeared. "Killian."

My boss frowned. "Remi. You okay?"

I nodded. "I have a rental in SoHo that's owned by a fake company. Can you trace the owner?"

"I can try." Killian steepled his hands. "You ready to explain yet?"

"I can't. I'm protecting you."

Kill growled. "Let me help you, Remi."

Mav leaned in. "You can help by looking up Zaria Corp."

"Fine." Killian's hawkish face hardened. "If I find something, I'll call. And Remi, if you need me, I'm only a call away."

"Thanks, Killian."

Mav scowled at the empty screen. "He's possessive of you."

"He's my boss. He looks out for everyone who works for him. He helped us out yesterday." Mav looked put out, so I kissed him. "What do we do now?"

"I'm going to call Zane and Liam for help."

A moment later, Mav had Zane on the screen. The billionaire was sitting in his office, an amazing view of the city behind him.

"Why are you in your office?" Mav asked.

"Last-minute meeting. You two okay?"

"We tracked The Shadow to a place in SoHo. It's owned by a shell company called Zaria Corp." Mav told him the address. "I thought you and Liam might be able to help."

"Do *not* go over there, Mav."

"We might need to—"

"That's not in your skill set. But, I have some visitors."

Two men stepped into view.

One was long, lanky, with long, dark hair pulled back in a stubby ponytail. The other held his muscled body in a way that signaled readiness. He had ink-black hair and dark-blue eyes that looked like they missed nothing. Both men were hot, but the black-haired one sent a chill down my spine.

"Remi, this is Ace Oliveira and Vander Norcross. Vander owns Norcross Security in San Francisco, and Ace is his tech guy."

Oh, the boogeyman's boogeyman.

Ace smiled, and I could see he was a bit of a charmer. But as I looked at the ruggedly handsome Vander Norcross, I thought badass-who-could-kill-you-with-one-finger might be a better title.

"Um...hi."

16

REPERCUSSIONS

Mav

"Vander, what are you doing in New York?" Mav asked.

"I had some work to do for Roth, here. Ace and I flew over. I was already worried when you texted to tell me about The Shadow. Then Zane told me everything else that's been going on." Vander shot an inscrutable look at Remi.

Ace lifted a tablet. "The company that owns the house listed in SoHo is offshore. Caymans."

Mav frowned. "So, a foreign owner?"

"Maybe, maybe not." Ace shrugged a shoulder. "It's a favorite place for good, old-fashioned American bad guys to hide assets, as well."

Vander crossed his arms. "You have no idea who you're dealing with?"

"We're trying to find out who," Remi said.

"He wants one of my company's military projects,"

Mav said. "That's not happening. He's also tried to killed Remi's family, and shot at us."

Vander and Ace traded a look.

"Let us look into it," Vander said.

Mav released a breath. "Okay."

"Sit tight. We'll get back to you soon."

Mav considered getting Rollo involved, but he had a nagging feeling. He didn't want Rollo in the middle of this mess, as well. Vander and Ace were better equipped to deal with it.

Remi paced, her moves jerky. "So, we just wait? I hate waiting."

"You might have mentioned that before. Vander, and his man, Ace, are good. Beyond good."

"I get that. Vander looks like he could personally take down a small army before dinner without breaking a sweat."

Mav's lips twitched.

"He's the kind of man who gives a woman ideas, but deep down, she knows she could never tame him."

Mav frowned. He didn't want Remi thinking about Vander at all, let alone taming him.

Remi's phone rang, and she snatched it up. She touched the speaker button. "Hello?"

A robotic voice filled the space. "You made the wrong choice, Rogue Angel."

Mav watched anger flare on her face. *Fuck.* How the hell had the guy gotten her new number?

"You tried to kill my family! You shot at us! You're a criminal. If you think I'm doing anything for you, you're crazy."

"There will be repercussions."

Now Mav saw the flash of fear in her eyes and his hand curled into a fist. He was tired of The Shadow toying with Remi and making her afraid.

"No, there won't be—" she snapped "—because we'll find you. You—"

The Shadow hung up.

"Dammit." She threw the phone and it hit the desk with a clatter.

Mav wrapped his arms around her from behind.

"I want all this to be over, Mav."

Her words were like a blow. Did she mean what was between them as well? He tried to tell himself it wasn't about him. She was scared, worried about her family.

Right then, she turned, pressing deeper against him and he realized he wanted to keep her exactly in that place.

Wanted to keep her. Period.

Sensation washed through him, and it wasn't exactly comfortable.

A word beginning with L reared its head.

Fuck.

"You hungry?" he growled.

She looked up. "What's wrong?"

"Nothing."

She rolled her eyes. "Pull the tough guy routine, then, but yes, I could eat."

He led her out of the lab and down to the kitchen and lounge. He watched her ooh over the snack selection. She snagged another cookie, a packet of M&Ms, and an apple.

She crunched into the apple, leaning back on one of the long tables. "This cancels out the candy."

"I don't think it works like that." He watched her. "When we get back, after all of this is over, I want to take you out to dinner."

She choked a little. "I'm staying with you. Of course, we'll have dinner."

"No. Out."

She lowered the apple. "Like a date?"

"Yes. And we'll have lunch with my parents."

Her nose wrinkled. "Mav—"

"And once your family is home safely, I want us to get away. Just us. Beach. Cabin. Winery. Wherever you'd like to go."

She blinked, then licked her lips. "Mav, this—" she waved a hand between them "—is not going to last."

An ugly sensation cut through him and he scowled.

"We're having a hot affair. Hot sex. It'll burn out." She gave him a strained smile. "I know that Hannah woman did a number on you, but one day, some pretty, smart socialite who dresses well, and goes to...I don't know, charity lunches, will catch your eye."

He growled. "You really believe that bullshit?"

"No," she growled. "But I have to, because I'm a foster kid from Brooklyn, thrown away by my parents, and several foster families before Mama, and I'm a hacker for a living. You're—" her gaze ran over him "—amazing. You can have anyone you want. Someone with an excellent pedigree and style."

Mav crossed his arms over his chest. "Seems I want you."

She closed her eyes. "It'll pass. It always does." She met his gaze, and he saw such sadness it made his bones ache. "People seem to have no trouble walking away from me."

"Remi—" His phone rang and he cursed. "It's Vander."

She nodded, and moved up beside him, but he noted that she was careful not to touch him.

Dammit. He'd deal with that later. He'd get it through her thick skull that she was *his*. He didn't care where she came from.

Mav put the call on speaker. "Hey, Vander, we're here."

"I'm here with Ace." The man's tone was dark and it made the hairs rise on the back of Mav's neck.

"Whoever owns that SoHo place is a ghost," Ace said. "Owns some other places around the country. All in the larger cities."

"Bolt holes," Mav mused.

"Yeah," Vander agreed. "I want to know who this asshole is."

"What do you suggest?" Mav asked.

"Ace and I are going to go in and take a look around the SoHo property."

Mav glanced at Remi. She was fiddling with her packet of M&Ms. "Okay, when?"

"Now," Vander replied. "We need thirty minutes to prep. We'll do some surveillance. If the place is empty, we'll go in."

"How will you know no one's home?" Remi asked.

"Easy," Ace said. "Get pizza delivered and see if anyone answers the knock."

"We'll also scan with an infrared camera attached to a drone," Vander added.

Mav wondered what the hell Vander packed in his bag when he traveled. He glanced at his watch. There was no time for him and Remi to get back to the city before Ace and Vander made their move.

"All right. Good luck, and keep us posted."

Remi

I bounced my foot, trying to control my nerves.

Mav put a big hand on my knee. "It'll be fine."

I nodded, sitting back in the computer lab chair.

Vander and Ace were getting ready to break into The Shadow's property. Right now, they were pulling up outside.

"In position." Vander's deep voice came through the computer speaker. He was wearing an earpiece.

"Scanning with thermal camera," Ace murmured.

I chewed on my lip.

"Clear," Vander said. "Initiating entry."

For a split second, panic flared. I turned to look at Mav. "He'll have an alarm."

"Ace can handle it. He's former NSA."

"Screw this." I couldn't handle not knowing what was going on. I tapped on the keyboard, and data flowed and flashed.

"What are you doing?" Mav asked.

"I want to see what's going on. I'm hacking into CCTV in the area."

Mav made a sound. I looked up and saw he was shaking his head, but he was smiling.

I kept working. "There."

On one of the screens, several images of the SoHo street popped up.

"That's the building there." Mav pointed.

I leaned forward, staring at the dark gray house. "I don't see Vander or Ace."

Mav snorted. "You won't. Have you heard of Ghost Ops?"

I shook my head.

"Teams are made up of the best of the best of special forces operators across all branches of the military. Delta force, Navy SEALs, Army Rangers, Green Beret, Marine Recon."

I felt a small shiver go down my spine.

"These teams are made of the toughest, baddest men who did the toughest, baddest jobs."

"Vander was Ghost Ops," I whispered.

"Commander of a Ghost Ops team."

King of the badasses. I wondered just what kind of woman would catch the attention of a man like that.

"We're in," Vander murmured.

Wow, he was good. I tapped my nails on the desk. When this was over, and The Shadow was behind bars, I was going to paint my nails a nice selection of pretty pastels to celebrate.

Mav turned my chair to face his, his legs on either side of mine.

"We didn't finish talking before, in the kitchen."

Oh, no. The guy was going to wear me down, reel me in, and then, when he finally moved on, I'd be a heartbroken shell. No, a heartbroken amoeba. Just a blob of sadness.

I refused to meet his gaze. "We did."

He gripped my chin. There was anger in his eyes.

"You're angry at me?" I whispered.

"No, I'm angry at life. At the things that made you doubt what's between us."

I went still. *Oh, God.* He was serious.

"Mav—"

"Remi, I get it. After Hannah, I shut myself off. Looking back, it wasn't so much because I loved her. I doubt we'd still be together today. She was nice, sweet, and what I thought I wanted at the time. It was more that she broke my trust. After, I doubted myself, my own judgment."

I leaned in and touched his leg. "We're all human, Mav. Even you."

"I know. It took me a while to accept."

My lips twitched.

"But the situation, it damaged my trust in myself. In opening up and taking risks again."

I looked away, my chest tight.

"Life did that to you, too," he said.

"I don't hold back. I love Mama, my family—"

"I know, but I'd guess that took a long time. A part of you is still reluctant to take the risk."

I swallowed. "Look at us, two relationship-phobes with trust issues."

He gave me that sexy smile that I loved, and I watched it unfurl on his rugged face.

Loved.

Oh, shit.

"I'm asking you to give us a chance," Mav continued. "After we deal with The Shadow."

"Mama needs her surgery—"

"And I want to be there to hold your hand. I'm going to prove to you that this, us, is worth taking the risk and facing our fears."

My throat closed. "Mav."

Suddenly, the lights went out.

We were plunged into darkness.

"God," I said with a gasp.

"It's okay." He took my hand. "We have backup power."

A second later, the lights blinked back on, and the computer screens followed.

Mav touched the keyboard. "Ruben?"

A harried-looking Ruben appeared on screen. "Sorry, we had a power surge from warehouse two. The backup power is on."

"Tisdale?"

Ruben scowled. "It could've been him. They haven't caught him yet. They've spotted him again inside the fence."

"So he's here inside the park?" Mav asked, brows drawing together in a fierce scowl.

"Yes, but security is chasing him."

"Keep me posted."

I turned back to the CCTV feed. I wondered what the hell Vander and Ace had found.

I stared at the unassuming building in SoHo.

Mav pulled me in, and pressed a quick kiss to my temple. "This will all be over soon."

As we waited, I sent a text to Mama.

I got an instant response. The kids were good, she was fine, and Boone was an excellent chess player.

Is your boy taking good care of you?

I laughed.

Mav stroked a hand over my hair. "What?"

"Mama just called you a boy."

He looked amused.

We're good. Miss you.

I tapped the desk again, and hoped that Vander and Ace were okay.

"Do I need to find a way to keep you busy, so you don't stress?" Mav asked.

I wrinkled my nose. Then I noticed a flicker on the screen, in one of the windows of the building. I frowned.

"What is it?" Mav asked.

I leaned in. "I...nothing. I thought I saw something in that window."

Suddenly, Vander's tense voice cut through the quiet. "Abort. *Abort.*"

Oh, no. I straightened, and Mav did, too.

"Something's wrong," Mav said.

Then the house exploded.

I cried out, watching the screen with horror.

Windows shattered, spraying glass. Smoke and flames billowed, and for a second, I was back standing in front of Mama's burning house.

That was what I'd seen. A flicker of flames in the window.

I grabbed Mav's hand, my gaze locked on the screen.

God, Vander and Ace.

All we could do was watch the fire burn.

17

HE WOULDN'T LEAVE ME

Mav

F uck. *Fuck.*
      Mav yanked out his phone. The lights on the ceiling flickered, then steadied.

He pressed the button and called Zane.

"Mav. *Shit.*" Zane's voice was tense. "Liam and I are parked on the street here. We called 9-1-1."

"Vander?"

"No sign yet. Hold tight." Zane ended the call.

"Oh, my God." Remi was pale faced. On the CCTV, they watched the fire intensify.

The Shadow wasn't playing around.

Mav tapped his foot on the floor. They'd underestimated this bastard. And right now, he just prayed that Vander and Ace were okay.

Mav pulled Remi into his lap.

"What if—?"

"Shh," he said. "It'll take more than some traitorous asshole to take out Vander Norcross."

"The Shadow won't stop, Mav. We're all in danger. You, my family."

He pressed a hand to the back of her neck and squeezed. "I'm mean, and I have resources. We will take him down. I promise. I won't let him hurt you, or any of your family."

The computer chimed with a call. Mav swiped the screen.

Zane was sitting in the front seat of his car. Behind him, in the backseat, Ace and Vander came into view.

Relief punched through Mav, and he heard Remi let out a hard breath.

Ace's long hair was loose and tangled, brushing his shoulders. Vander had a smudge of black on his cheek.

And Vander was angry. Icily angry.

"You okay?" Mav asked.

Vander gave a curt nod. "We got out a window in time."

"What happened?" Remi asked.

"The place was rigged to blow," Ace said.

"At first, it looked normal," Vander said. "Like someone lived there. But something felt off."

"Staged," Ace said.

"But we did get into a locked office." Vander ran a hand through his hair. "And a safe I don't think we were supposed to find. I'm guessing the asshole figured it would go up in the explosion."

The tone of Vander's voice made Mav's insides go cold. "You found something."

"Your guy is organized, keeps good records. I found a list of the jobs he's done."

"Jobs?" Remi frowned. "Like hacking jobs?"

"No, The Shadow is a jack-of-all-trades."

"So, he isn't a foreign government, or a terrorist?" Mav asked.

"No, but he sells to them. He's someone who sells to the highest bidder. He carries out impossible, high-risk jobs—steals items, espionage, and doesn't just acquire hard-to-reach info."

"Vander," Mav growled. "What aren't you telling us?"

"He's an assassin."

"What?" Remi's eyes went wide.

"A good one." Vander's gaze bored into Mav's. "Mav, you and Remi need to get back to the city, and we'll get you to a secure location."

Remi sucked in a breath. Mav ground his teeth together. "What did you find?"

"He knows this job has gone bad, and he's the kind of man to tidy up loose ends. He's coming after you and Remi."

"*Fuck*. Okay, we'll head back now."

He had to keep Remi safe. That was all that mattered.

Suddenly Vander's image distorted.

"Mav... You... Fast..."

Dammit. "Vander, you're breaking up." Mav tapped the keyboard. "Wait, I'll—"

They were plunged into darkness.

Remi gripped his arm. "What happened to the backup power? Um, this isn't good, right?"

"Right." Mav pulled out his cell phone, and turned on the flashlight function. It bathed them in a bluish-white glow.

Faint lights were still lit up on the floor. The emergency lighting.

"The backup power is gone."

She lifted her chin and swallowed. "He's here, isn't he?"

"Maybe." Mav looked at his phone. "No signal."

She frowned. "You think he's jamming us?"

"Yeah."

"Does the emergency power run the computer system?" she asked.

He shook his head. "Only the emergency security terminal in the main security hub will be active."

"So we go there."

Or they could hide here, and hunker down. Mav hated the idea of doing nothing, but keeping her safe was his top priority.

Hell. But this asshole was hunting them.

"Wait." He pulled his phone out again. "We have an internal comms system." He checked. "It's still operational."

He touched a contact.

Ruben's face came up on the small screen.

"Ruben, I think we have a dangerous assassin on site."

"What?" His head of operations squeezed the bridge

of his nose. "God, you throw some interesting curveballs at me, Mav. You aren't joking?"

"No."

"Are you safe?"

"We're thinking about getting to the security hub. Get the power back on, and call for help."

"Shit." Ruben paused for a second. "Look, I'm closer to the hub. The damn security team is out chasing Tisdale."

Mav paused. Hell, had The Shadow somehow arranged that?

"I'll make my way there and contact you again," Ruben said.

"Thanks, Ruben."

"No problem, I—"

There was a flash of movement, followed by a grunt, and a shout. Ruben's phone skidded across the floor.

"Oh, no," Remi gasped.

They now had a view of the wall, and Mav heard the sounds of a fight, then nothing.

"Ruben? Ruben?"

Fuck. Dammit.

A black-gloved hand came into view. The call cut off.

Remi was breathing fast.

"Get your phone," Mav bit out. "We have to go."

Her teeth sank into her bottom lip. "Wouldn't it be safer to stay here?"

Mav understood the urge to hide. To stay safe.

"He's coming for us. We need to get to the hub."

She pressed a shaky hand to her face.

"Trust me?" Mav asked.

She hugged him. "Yes."

"Let's go."

Mav lifted the panel beside the door. The electronic lock was dead, but beneath it was a manual door control.

He heard the click, then the door opened.

He took her hand.

Out in the hallway, blue emergency lighting glowed, giving the place an eerie feel.

They moved quietly down the corridor, then turned a corner. Ahead was a wall of windows. The sun was setting, flooding the back in orange-gold light.

Remi's fingers clenched on his.

"This way," he whispered.

A noise echoed from somewhere deeper in the complex, and they froze.

Nothing moved.

Shit. Mav wished he had a weapon. He pulled Remi closer.

"Come on." He tugged her out of the atrium and down the hall.

They needed to get to the security hub.

***

Remi

I was freaked.

My heart pounded and my mouth was dry.

An assassin was hunting us. It felt unreal. Like a horror movie, or bad dream.

Mav squeezed my fingers and I released a breath.

I wasn't alone, and I knew he wouldn't leave me.

My chest locked. He wouldn't leave me. That certainty rocketed through me.

"Down here," Mav whispered.

He towed me down another corridor. It was so dark, but thankfully empty. I swallowed. We had to get that call out.

There was a door at the end. Mav tried it, but it was locked, and he muttered a curse.

"Let me." I connected my phone to the lock, and tapped.

Beep. The door opened.

Inside was a large kitchen and dining area. It was much larger than the one near Mav's private lab.

We skirted the long rows of tables.

Then I heard a noise coming from the opposite side of the room.

"Down," he whispered urgently.

I dropped to the floor, crouching by a table. My heartbeat echoed in my ears.

Mav pointed.

Through the legs of the chairs, I saw a dark shadow moving at the edge of the room. I soundlessly sucked in a breath.

It was *him*. The Shadow. The person who'd caused all this trouble.

And for what? Money? Greed?

The Shadow was a man who stole and killed, for his own benefit.

I looked at Mav in the gloom.

He was the opposite. A man who also made so much

money, but by creating, allowing his employees to collaborate and invent needed tech.

The Shadow disappeared. God, where was he? My pulse was racing so fast that I was worried my chest would burst open.

After a long moment, Mav nodded. We rose and continued onward.

We slipped down another hall. That's when I saw a dark form on the floor.

"*Ruben*," Mav said.

We rushed to the man and dropped to our knees. I watched Mav feel for a pulse and I touched Ruben's head. I felt something sticky.

Oh no. *Blood*.

Mav released a harsh breath. "He's alive."

"What do we do?" We couldn't carry him out of here.

"Put him on his side. The best thing to help him, is to get to the hub and call for help."

I nodded. I helped him gently roll Ruben onto his side. I unbuttoned Ruben's shirt and maneuvered it off him, leaving him in a T-shirt. I used the shirt to staunch the bleeding, tucking the fabric under his head.

"Hold on," I whispered.

Mav pulled me up.

We jogged down the hall, and I stayed close behind him.

He paused, listening. "Almost there."

We rounded another corner, and picked up speed.

"That door." He pointed.

I saw it. It had an emergency light above it and the sign was marked *Security*. I felt a rush of giddy relief.

Suddenly, a tall form shot out of a doorway right at us.

Mav knocked me back and I swallowed a cry.

Mav moved and rammed a punch at the man, then grabbed him and slammed him against the wall.

"Mr. Rivera!"

Mav stilled. "Tisdale?"

The disgruntled employee.

"I didn't do this." The man swallowed. "I only wanted to help."

He was thin, pale-faced, with greasy, dirty-blond hair. He swallowed again and his large Adam's apple bobbed.

"I know, Tisdale," Mav said. "You need to hide. There's a dangerous person in the building."

The man's eyes went wide. "The Russians?"

Mav sighed. "I don't think so."

"The Chinese?"

"No," Mav growled. "Look. Can you hide until I come and get you?"

Tisdale straightened. "I want to help."

"Great, let's—"

There was a sound behind us. A scraping. It echoed down the hall.

My heart jumped into my throat and I spun. I didn't see anyone in the darkness. "Mav, we have to hurry."

Tisdale stepped forward. "I can lure him away."

"Tisdale, *no*." Mav lunged, but the man took off, surprisingly fast. "Fuck."

"Helllllooo," Tisdale yelled, disappearing around the corner.

I saw that Mav wanted to go after him. "The best way to help him is to call the police."

Mav nodded.

We reached the door to the hub. I connected to it and tried to hack it. I frowned. "It's not working."

"Security rooms have enhanced security." Mav's jaw tightened. He opened the panel, and yanked the wires out. He fiddled, and connected some.

The door opened.

So much for enhanced security.

Mav shot me a look. "Yeah, I know. Not the problem right now."

I shrugged in reply as we hustled into the room. Mav slid a deadbolt across the door behind us.

Inside looked like a standard security office, complete with a wall of screens. They were currently blank.

I sat in one of the chairs. "Okay, let's do this."

Mav pressed his hand to a scanner. It beeped and the system unlocked, the main screen flaring to life.

"Hmm." I frowned. I needed to find the power system for the building. "Where's the power system?"

He rattled off where I needed to go and I tapped quickly.

"I like watching you work," he said.

I glanced at him. "Hey, no flirting. At least, not while a deadly assassin is after us."

His teeth were white in the low light.

I lost myself in the system. Ah, I saw what the asshole had done.

There.

I tapped the Enter key. The lights came on.

"You *did* it," Mav said.

Security screens flickered to life one by one. I saw lights coming on in different spaces around Rivera Tech Park. I could see that outside, night was falling.

"Look," Mav pointed.

I saw the assassin. He had his back to the camera and was dressed in black. His hair was black as well, and he had a mask over the lower portion of his face.

He raised a handgun.

Oh, no. I saw Tisdale running.

I couldn't hear the report of the gun, but I imagined it.

Tisdale fell.

Mav cursed. "We need to stop his jamming and make the call."

"On it." I looked back at the computer screen. My fingers flew. *Come on.*

This asshole couldn't be as good as Mav and me.

Mav was tapping on the other desktop.

"I can't stop the jamming," I said. "However he's doing it, it isn't through your system."

"We need to block the frequency he's using." Mav stood and started yanking things out of the cabinets.

He pulled out some items, found a screwdriver. Next, he yanked out some electronics. He muttered as he joined wires and pulled parts of things and joined them together.

On the screen, I saw the assassin head into a corridor.

The next second, he was gone.

My insides crawled. "Mav, I lost him." I frantically searched the screens.

Where the hell did he go?

Then I saw a flicker of movement, and glimpsed him. Bile rose in my throat. "Mav, he's coming this way!"

"Okay, hang on." He plugged his makeshift device into the computer.

He thumbed the keyboard—Mav's fingers didn't dance, they punched.

I heard a ping. I smiled. "Jamming is down, we have phone signal!"

He leaned down and pressed a hard kiss on my lips.

Then Mav yanked his cell phone out and tapped in a text.

"I'm texting Zane. Now for 9-1-1—" he pressed the phone to his ear. "Yes, it's an emergency. I'm Maverick Rivera, and I'm at Rivera Tech Park. We have a security breach, and a murderer on site."

I half listened as he spoke to the 9-1-1 operator.

On-screen, I saw the assassin getting closer.

"Mav, he's *coming.*"

Mav swiveled and looked at the screen.

"He can't get in, right?"

A muscle ticked in Mav's jaw.

"Right."

"Fuck, we can't take that risk." He shoved his phone into his pocket. "We have to move."

18

JUMP AND LIVE

Mav

Mav kept a tight grip on Remi's hand as they exited the security hub.

Help was coming. They just had to hold on until it arrived.

"Where to?" Remi whispered.

"Outside. We'll find a place to hide."

Cautiously, they navigated the corridors and crept out into the main atrium. Night had well and truly fallen.

It was dark outside, but at least the lights were on inside. He paused and scanned. There was no sound.

He pulled her forward. He needed to get her safe. The refrain was a drumbeat in his head.

Get out of the building. That was the goal.

He turned, moving past a huge glass wall that cordoned off a hall and an open area filled with plants.

"*Mav.*"

At her whisper, his head jerked up and he followed the direction of her gaze.

A tall man strode across the space, a gun aimed at them.

"Run!" Mav roared.

He and Remi sprinted.

Gunfire echoed loudly in the atrium. Remi screamed.

The glass wall shattered.

"*Faster*." He shoved her ahead.

More bullets slammed into the wall behind them.

Mav leaped over a table. He saw Remi drop to the floor, crawling. The assassin was advancing on them.

Mav grabbed a chair and lifted it off the ground.

"Our deaths achieve nothing," Mav said. "We've already shared everything we know about you with the authorities."

The Shadow shrugged. "I'm The Shadow, and I don't leave loose ends." He glanced Remi's way. "And I don't let anyone play me."

He had dark eyes, but the mask covered the rest of his face. There was no discernible accent in his voice. Mav suspected he wouldn't recognize him in a crowd.

Mav swung the chair and tossed it at the assassin.

Next, Mav spun and yanked Remi up, shielding her.

They sprinted across the atrium, running toward a closed door. Mav hit the crash bar hard with his arm.

It didn't open.

"Mav—"

More gunfire behind them.

Fuck. He grabbed her arm and ran into the kitchen.

They ducked down behind a long bench. They needed another exit.

"There's a back way," he said, kissing her quickly. "We need to get out the door. Run as fast as you can. There's a short hall, run past the fridges. Then you'll see the outside exit."

"You're coming too," she said.

"I'll distract him first. Go!"

She took two steps. The assassin charged in, firing wildly.

Mav ducked back down, and prayed that Remi stayed down and got out. That was all that mattered.

Ahead of him, Mav spotted frying pans stacked on shelves under the counter. He grabbed two heavy cast-iron ones.

He leaped up and threw one of the frying pans.

It hit the assassin in the shoulder and the man cursed. Mav leaped onto the counter, slid over, then swung the second frying pan at the man.

It hit the man's arm and gun, sending the weapon flying. It disappeared under the kitchen counters.

But The Shadow yanked out a second one.

Fuck.

"Ahh!"

Mav turned his head and his chest filled with concrete. Remi ran along the counter, and jumped.

She held a spray can of cooking oil in her hand. She aimed the aerosol at the assassin's face.

The man grunted and threw his arms up for protection.

"Come on!" She grabbed Mav's hand, and they sprinted back into the dining room.

"I told you to get out," he growled.

"I know. I didn't listen." Her golden-brown gaze met his—fierce, defiant. "I like you, big guy. That asshole doesn't get to hurt you."

Fuck. *Fuck.* Emotion stormed through Mav.

They ran and turned down another corridor. Behind them, he heard running footsteps.

"He's coming," she said.

Damn.

Ahead was a wall covered in greenery. One part was draped in vines.

"Here." He dived into a tight space behind the plants, and pulled Remi in against him. He let the vines fall back into place.

Her wide eyes met his and he saw her fear. He stroked her jaw.

Footsteps.

They both tensed.

The Shadow stopped, just a few feet away from their hiding place.

Shit. Did he know they were there?

Then the assassin walked down the hall and his footsteps faded.

Remi sagged against Mav. They waited. They waited some more. He was tempted to stay there. How far away were the damn police?

But he and Remi couldn't stay here. The fucker was smart, and he'd eventually double back and work out where they were hiding.

Mav peered out, then pulled Remi into the empty hallway.

They hurried back the way they'd come, and then up some stairs to the mezzanine level. There were lots of doors.

One was labeled Testing Lab.

"I hear him," she whispered.

Sure enough, footsteps sounded below. Heading up the stairs.

Fuck.

"Hack the lock," Mav said.

She lifted her phone and set to work.

Come on. Come on.

The door lock flashed, and they slipped inside.

"Now jam it."

Nodding, she tapped on her phone. "Got it," she whispered.

Seconds later, someone tried the handle from the outside, jiggling it.

Remi gasped and slapped her hand over her mouth.

Mav scanned the darkened lab. There were benches covered in various pieces of equipment, and he spied a computer. He pulled the keyboard out and logged on. He tapped.

There. He'd accessed the security system.

The assassin was in the hall, trying to hack the door lock.

Damn, they were sitting ducks.

"I have an idea." Remi shouldered him aside.

Her fingers flew in a complicated dance. With a

smile, she tapped the screens, and outside in the hall, the fire sprinklers erupted, dousing The Shadow with water.

On-screen, Mav saw the man cursing. His dark hair was plastered to his head, his clothes soaking.

Mav laughed and pressed a kiss to her temple. "Damn, I love you."

She went still, like a woodland creature who'd spotted a predator.

"You look more scared of me than the assassin chasing us," he said dryly.

"Mav—" A taut whisper filled with so much emotion.

He loved this woman. This smart, spunky, loyal woman.

He'd convince her of that after they got out alive.

The door shuddered.

He looked up.

The assassin had abandoned subtlety, and was now just trying to smash his way in.

Remi

There was nowhere to go.

My heart was doing a rapid dance against my ribs.

It was partly because of the assassin. And partly because Mav had just said he loved me.

I shook my head and scanned the room.

"Hey, over there." There was a door.

We raced over. It had a tiny glass window embedded

in it. I peered into it and my stomach dropped. "It is a storage room. Mav, there's no way out of here."

Maybe the assassin wouldn't get in. I looked at the security feed again.

I frowned. "What's he doing?"

Mav cursed, staring at the small objects in The Shadow's hand. "Those are small, localized explosives."

My heart leaped up, trying to choke me. "He's going to *blow* the door down?"

Mav scanned the room again, his face hard. He looked back at the storage room.

"I need you to fry that lock."

I frowned. "What? Why?"

"We're going to let him think we're in the storage room."

"Okay," I said slowly.

"It has a secondary lockdown door. They store dangerous chemicals in there. The secondary door slams closed if there's a breach."

My mind raced, then I grinned. "We can trap him in there."

He nodded. "Do it, angel."

I raced to the computer and accessed the storage room doors. I glanced at the feed. *Crap.* He was almost done.

"I've got control of the secondary door, and..."

Poof. The lights on the door lock died.

I spun around to see Mav on a chair. He was pushing a ceiling tile upward.

"Come on. Hurry." He held his hand out to me.

Mouth dry, I ran over. He gripped my waist and

lifted me like I weighed nothing. I grabbed the edge of the hole in the ceiling and climbed inside.

"Stay on the beams or you'll fall through," he warned.

Oh, great.

Mav climbed up behind me, just as I heard a muffled thump down below. Mav set the ceiling tile back in place.

I held my breath and leaned against Mav. His big presence steadied me.

I heard more sounds below, then a muttered curse and more movements. What was he doing? Was he trying to get into the store room?

Mav tapped on his phone and held it out to me.

It was a bad view, but the camera just caught the shoulder of the assassin.

He was pressing something to the storage room door.

I tried to keep my breathing calm.

God. What if he had even more of those explosives? The room wouldn't trap him for long.

I heard the thumps of the next explosions. On the small screen, the door fell down.

The assassin spun and strode into the storage room.

"Now!" Mav ordered.

I thumbed my phone.

The secondary door clanged shut.

I sucked in a breath. "We did it!"

Mav shoved the ceiling tile across, then leaped down.

He motioned for me to follow. With no hesitation, I jumped right into his arms.

We turned.

The furious eyes of The Shadow were right in the

glass window in the storage room door. I felt a skitter of dread.

This was a man who'd never stop.

I got a sense that it wasn't just about the money. This man liked his work.

"Come on." Mav yanked me out of the room. "He might have more of those explosives."

God, I hoped not.

We raced out the door. The sprinklers were still on, drenching us. I almost slipped on the slick floor.

Mav's hand tightened on mine, holding me up. He kept moving across the mezzanine and finally we reached the edge of the sprinklers. I'd only activated the ones outside the lab.

I pushed my wet hair out of my face. A huge net draped down from the ceiling, covered in green climbing plants, all the way to the floor below.

It looked like a green waterfall.

"You will die here."

The shout made my adrenaline spike and I glanced back.

The assassin was striding toward us, his lean body moving fast. His black hair was plastered to his head.

He held a massive knife with a jagged blade in his hand.

Oh. God. We'd never make it to the stairs in time.

Mav stopped and looked at the green net.

"Jump," he said.

I shook my head, my brain not computing.

He lifted me onto the railing.

"Mav, no—"

"Jump and live! Stay and he'll get us."

Dammit.

I didn't let myself think. "You're jumping too."

"Right behind you, angel. I promise."

The Shadow was almost on us.

I dragged in a deep breath. I wanted to live. I wanted Mav.

I'd been protecting myself, holding back.

Not anymore.

I lifted my chin and leaped.

There was a moment of weightlessness, then I slammed into the net and grabbed onto the leaves. Greenery hit my face and the net swung a little.

A second later, Mav hit it. This time, it swung wildly under his larger weight.

Oh, shit. I almost slipped, and tightened my grip.

"Down," Mav yelled.

I started downward. He moved quicker than me.

Suddenly, the entire net swayed and I looked up.

My gut clenched. The assassin had followed us.

"Keep moving, Remi," Mav ordered.

I hustled. Below me, Mav reached the bottom.

Only a few more feet.

The net swung. The assassin tried to kick me.

I let go, and I fell the last few feet.

Oh, God.

I landed on my butt with a hard jolt. Mav yanked me up.

A dark shape fell from above. Unlike me, the assassin landed gracefully in an elegant crouch, one long leg outstretched to the side.

Mav and I backed up.

The Shadow rose. His mask was gone.

He had a fairly ordinary face, but with sharp cheekbones.

"I don't like to kill," he said. "I take no pleasure in it."

Bullshit. "So go," I said.

"No, it's my one rule. I finish what I start."

He walked toward us. The knife was so big.

Mav shoved me back.

God, he'd protect me. He'd get stabbed, he'd die for me.

I bit my lip. Pain and panic churned inside me.

The assassin darted forward, and then Mav *moved.*

My mouth dropped open.

He slammed a hard kick into The Shadow's mid-section, sending him staggering backward.

Mav could fight.

The men circled, attacking and blocking each other. Mav dodged the knife, and landed a punch.

I saw The Shadow's mouth tighten.

Mav attacked in a flurry of hits and kicks. One kick caught the assassin, and sent him crashing into a table.

"Not so easy when your prey fights back, is it?" Mav said.

"I always win, Mr. Rivera."

"So do I."

The men charged at each other. God, where were the police?

I had to help Mav. I scanned around and all I saw were empty tables.

No, wait.

One table had two laptops resting on it—one open, one closed. A coffee mug sat beside them. Someone had abandoned them, probably when the power went out.

The Shadow and Mav clashed again.

Mav grunted and jerked back.

I saw the cut on his bicep, the gash in his shirt.

And then I saw the blood.

19

YOU CHANGED EVERYTHING

Mav

The cut stung like hell.

Mav ignored it and focused on his opponent.

He tried to block Remi out, his worry for her. Simeon's voice echoed in his head. *Focus on your opponent. Their every move.*

People gave a lot away in a fight. In faint movements, the flicker of their eyes, the shift of their feet.

Mav had to keep Remi safe. The need beat inside him, steady like a drum.

Keep the woman he loved safe.

The Shadow attacked.

Mav released the breath in his lungs. He slammed his arm against the man's, blocking the slash of the knife.

He bent his knees and hammered his fist into the assassin's thigh.

The man's leg collapsed, but he was good. He leaped back and caught his balance.

They circled each other.

The Shadow jumped onto a table and ran at Mav, knife flashing. Mav dodged, gripped the man's shirt and yanked.

The assassin crashed to the ground and Mav got a kick in before The Shadow rolled away.

"Yeah, Mav, mess him up!" Remi yelled.

Hell. Even in the middle of a life-and-death fight, she made him want to laugh.

The assassin rose to his feet, cautious now, but angry.

Not a good combination.

They clashed again. Mav swung, grunted. He whipped his head to the side to avoid the knife, but paid for it with a fist to his gut.

Damn. He danced back. The asshole wasn't holding anything back.

Suddenly, The Shadow whipped something off his belt and tossed it.

Fuck. *Fuck*. A grenade.

"Remi, down!"

Mav saw her drop.

The grenade clattered to a stop.

Nothing happened.

Shit, decoy. Mav was already whirling, but The Shadow was on him.

The knife slid into Mav's side.

He met the man's dark gaze and saw him smile.

Mav felt the blood run down his flank.

"No!" Remi's scream made them both jerk.

The assassin stepped back, the blade sliding out of Mav.

He groaned. *Shit*. So much blood. He clutched his side.

He couldn't go down. He couldn't give up. He had to protect Remi.

The Shadow attacked again, and Mav blocked, and managed a front kick. But it was shaky. He was losing too much blood, and already feeling dizzy.

One leg went out from under him and he dropped to his knees.

He blinked at the blood on the floor.

The Shadow smiled, lifted the knife and advanced.

"*No!* You're not taking him from me."

Remi flew in, holding a laptop in her hand. She swung it like a bat.

It connected with The Shadow's head.

The man snarled and swung at her. She leaned back.

Not quite fast enough.

Shit, no. Mav saw the line of red across her chest.

With a growl, she swung the laptop again.

This time it slammed into the knife and the assassin dropped it to the tiles. She hit him again, and again. She smacked the assassin's head, chest.

"He's mine. You *don't* get to hurt him, asshole."

Mav smiled weakly. His Rogue Angel.

"You don't get to destroy more lives. I'm stopping you, right here, right now."

The Shadow ducked, but she kept bashing him, fueled by her fury. She swung the laptop hard at his head. *Crack.*

With a cry, he fell, crashing into a table.

The back of his head hit the edge and he collapsed to the floor.

Breathing heavily, Remi kicked the man.

He didn't move.

Good. Unable to hold himself up anymore, Mav tilted sideways and fell.

"*Mav.*" She raced to him. "Jesus, *God.*" She pressed her hands to his cheeks, then probed his side. "Stay with me."

He felt the energy draining out of him. She made a terrified sound, then whipped her shirt off, leaving her in a lacy, black bra.

As she pressed the balled-up shirt to his bleeding side, Mav grunted.

Damn, everything was starting to hurt now.

"Remi, I love you."

Her eyes filled. "You weren't supposed to do that. I thought you didn't believe in love?"

"I always have. My parents love each other so much. It's uncomfortable catching them kissing, in the kitchen, in the hall, in the yard."

Remi gave a hiccupping laugh. "It sounds sweet."

"After Hannah, I cut myself off from love, hardened my heart."

He lifted a hand to Remi's cheek. He managed to smear blood on her skin. "You changed everything. My Remi. My hacker. My angel."

A sob escaped her. "Oh God, Mav, I love you too." She gulped. "I've been terrified about falling for you. Worried you'd leave me and break my heart."

Like so many in her life had done.

"Never." He stroked her silky cheek. "I want to protect your heart."

"Well, despite you being a billionaire and having gazillions of dollars, I love you, Maverick Rivera."

"Some women like the billions."

She scowled. "Not me. I like your brain." She kissed his forehead. "And your friendly, open personality."

His lips quirked.

Then he saw movement behind her.

His breath froze in his chest. "*Remi.*"

She spun.

The Shadow rose. There was blood on his face. He scooped up the knife off the floor, and started toward them.

No. Mav tried to move, but his body wouldn't obey.

Remi tensed, hovering over him protectively.

She had no weapon.

Fuck.

Suddenly, he heard a high-pitched whine. Then all the walls of glass in the atrium shattered.

Four men in black body armor burst into the huge space.

They raced toward them, holding black assault rifles up and aimed.

Vander stepped forward, face set and hard behind his rifle. "Drop it."

The Shadow looked at the men, then dropped his knife.

"Boone," Vander said.

Mav recognized Boone's tall form. The man yanked out plastic cuffs and advanced on The Shadow.

"Clear," a deep voice called.

One of the other men had circled around, checking for any more enemies.

Remi gasped. "Killian?"

Her boss nodded at her.

The fourth man, Ace, lowered his rifle and pulled out a tablet. "Okay, let me get the cops in here."

Vander and Killian crouched beside Remi and Mav.

"Help him, please," she said.

Killian slid a backpack off. He pulled out a first aid kit.

"Hang in there, Rivera." Her boss started working on Mav's wound.

"The asshole hacked the security gates," Ace said. "The police have been stuck at the front gate." Ace smiled. "There."

Seconds later, the wail of sirens split the air.

There was the noise of an internal door opening.

The four men whipped their rifles up. A man with a wild cloud of brown hair and large eyes stumbled in, a half-eaten candy bar in his hand. He froze, looking at the guns. Then he dropped his gaze to Mav.

"Mav-man, you're bleeding."

Mav let out a strangled laugh. "I know, Rollo."

"Shit." The man bit into his candy bar. "What did I miss?"

"A crazed assassin," Mav said.

Rollo nodded. "Cool."

Remi pressed her head to Mav's and held on. "Don't leave me."

"I'm not going anywhere, angel."

Remi

I was in love with Maverick Rivera.

It made all sorts of emotion swell inside me.

He loved me back.

We had survived.

We had beaten The Shadow.

I stayed close to Mav's side, my fingers tangled with his. I'd put my shirt back on and we were both covered in blood. I glanced over to where The Shadow was handcuffed on his knees and surrounded by police.

Vander and Boone were talking with the cops.

I heard Mav grunt in pain. Killian was still working on his wound.

"It's deep," Killian said.

"Hurts."

I clutched Mav's hand tighter. "Come on, tough guy. It's just a scratch."

He tried to smile, but slumped, his eyes closing.

"Mav. *Mav!*" Hot panic was slick inside me. "Killian!"

My boss cursed. "He's lost too much blood. We need the paramedics here."

"They're coming in now," someone called out.

My heart was racing like galloping horses. I leaned over Mav. "Don't you *dare* leave me, Maverick Rivera." Pain cleaved me open. God, maybe it was me. People just couldn't stay. "I love you, dammit, and you said you loved me." My voice broke.

Killian was focused on putting pressure on Mav's wound, but he sent me a look filled with sympathy.

"I love everything about you," I continued to whisper to Mav. I pressed my cheek to his hair. "Your brain, I told you that already. Your honesty. You don't pretend to be anything except who you are. I actually like your grumpiness. I like working with you. I like hot sex with you and your big—"

Killian made a choked noise.

Then I heard a low, pained chuckle.

"Mav?"

His gorgeous, brown eyes looked up at me. "I love you too, angel. It's going to be okay."

"Coming through!" a deep voice boomed.

The paramedics pushed in.

"Step back, ma'am," a man said.

"He needs blood," Killian said. "Stab wound to his left side—"

I got shoved back, and I watched them work on him.

I suddenly felt cold. I wrapped my arms around myself but it didn't help the shivers.

A strong arm wrapped around me and I looked up into Vander's rugged face. The man was hot, but he was still scary.

"He'll be fine. Mav doesn't let anything keep him down for long."

Boone appeared, holding a blanket, and he wrapped it around me.

"You're shaken up," Vander said. "It'll pass."

"Oh, I think I'm entitled. We were chased by a

crazed assassin, and my...man is hurt. I'm going to enjoy every second of my shock, thank you."

The corner of Vander's mouth twitched. "You'll be fine. I like you, Solano."

"I could probably like you too, but you kind of freak me out." I cocked my head. "How many ways do you know how to kill a man?"

He grinned, and the air got stuck in my lungs. Yep, Vander Norcross was hot.

"Too many." His smile vanished.

I glanced over and saw some other paramedics wheeling stretchers across the room. I spotted Ruben and Tisdale. "Are they okay?"

Vander nodded.

"Did The Shadow hurt anyone?"

"He killed a couple of security guards."

"Damn." I felt sorry for the families.

"Those two should be fine, though. The gunshot wound might be touch-and-go."

"Hey, she has a cut," Mav called out.

An older, grizzled paramedic nodded. "We'll get someone to deal with it."

"Now," Mav ordered.

I rolled my eyes. "Well, being stabbed hasn't diminished your bossiness."

He scowled at me. "I want you taken care of."

And dammit if that didn't make me feel mushy.

Then they loaded him onto a stretcher.

"We're on the move," a paramedic said.

I grabbed Mav's hand. Did his face have a bit more color in it? "You're going to be fine."

He scowled. "You're still bleeding."

"I'll get it dealt with. Stop fussing."

We reached the ambulance. The other paramedic, a competent woman about ten or fifteen years older than me, opened the doors.

I turned to Mav. "I'll see you at the hospital—"

"*No.*" Mav grabbed my hand. "You're coming with me."

"Mav—"

"Get on the stretcher."

"There's no room!"

His hold on my hand was like iron. "I'm not letting you go. I'm not leaving you."

My heart melted into a big pile of goo.

The female paramedic straightened. "Mr. Rivera—"

"My girlfriend is coming with us," he ordered.

I stilled. "Girlfriend?"

"Woman, I don't care which label you use." He tugged me closer, his palm to my cheek. "Mine."

Happy tears welled in my eyes.

The paramedic huffed. "I was going to say she can come, but you didn't let me finish. Nice speech, though."

I grinned at her. "It was, wasn't it? He's in love with me."

"I'd hold on to that one, honey."

I met Mav's gaze. "I think I might."

They loaded Mav in and I sat beside him. I wasn't ever letting go.

At the hospital, they finally made me let go, and whisked him into an examination room.

Jeez, my hands and clothes were covered in a lot of blood. I did *not* want to see myself in a mirror.

The doors burst open, and Zane and Liam rushed in, their women right behind them.

Uh-oh.

The men saw me and stumbled to a halt. Their gazes took in the blood, and they both looked speechless.

"Um, hi," I said.

Zane's gaze raked me, snagging on my hands. All the color left his face.

"Oh, it's fine. Mav's fine. He's got a stab wound, but —" I powered through the small hitch in my voice "—they said he'd be fine."

"Bloody hell." Liam released a breath.

"So that blood is Mav's?" Zane asked.

I swallowed and nodded. "Most of it. He's going to be fine. They said he'd be fine."

"Easy, Remi." Zane took my arm. "You said most of it. Is some of it yours?"

I blinked. "Maybe."

"Come on." He looked around. "Nurse, we need somewhere for her to clean up. And she has a nasty cut on her chest."

Wow, Zane's bossy tone was almost as good as Mav's.

The nurse's brows drew together.

Liam stepped in with a charming smile. "She needs that blood off her, and to get off her feet."

Dazzled, the nurse blinked. "Sure. Exam Three is free."

"That's my man," Aspen murmured with a grin.

Monroe took my other side. "Let's get you cleaned up."

"They said he'd be fine."

"Then he will be."

"I'm in love with him."

Monroe smiled. "I know."

"How do you handle being in love with a billionaire?"

"By remembering that you love the man under the billionaire most of all." Monroe met Zane's gaze and the pair shared a smile.

Then they hustled me into the exam room.

20

BILLIONAIRES KNOW HOW TO THROW A PARTY

Mav

"You're a lucky man, Mr. Rivera," the doctor said. The guy looked like he was fresh out of school until you looked into his eyes. They were tired, experienced, and a little weary.

"Yeah, I am."

"The stab wound was deep, but fortunately missed anything vital."

Mav nodded. He wasn't thinking about the wound. He was thinking about Remi.

Hell, he had a great family, thriving business, good friends... And now a woman he loved.

He smiled.

"Where is my son?" a loud voice said.

Uh-oh. His mom was in full-on mom mode.

His mother stormed in, followed by all of his family—including his brothers, sister, their partners, his niece and nephew. As usual, they were all talking at once.

"I'm fine," Mav said.

His mom took in his bare chest, the white bandage on his side, and the smears of blood that the nurse hadn't quite gotten rid of. Her lips trembled.

"Mom, come here." He hugged her. "I'm alive, I'm breathing."

"They... They said someone tried to *kill* you."

"Well, he didn't succeed. You should've seen Remi. She bashed the guy with a laptop."

Dad gripped Mav's shoulder. "Where is she?"

Mav frowned. "They shoved me in here and made her leave. I want to find her." He pushed up off the bed. He was attached by an IV to a bag of fluid, but it was on a stand on wheels. Looked like it was coming, too.

His mother frowned. "Maverick—"

"No. Mom, I love her. I'm going to marry her."

His mother gasped. His siblings and their offspring went silent.

Tears welled in his mother's eyes. She cupped his cheeks. "You finally opened up."

"More like she burrowed in without even trying. She is..." He couldn't find the words.

"You love her."

"Yeah."

His mother gave a decisive nod. "Then let's find her."

The entire Rivera clan mobilized.

Outside the exam room, he saw Vander, Ace, and Killian leaning against the wall. A small huddle of nurses was eyeing the trio with hungry, speculative looks.

Vander met Mav's gaze, and lifted his chin.

"Mom, this is Vander and his man, Ace. They

rescued us. And this is Killian Hawke, Remi's boss. He helped, as well." Mav frowned. "How the hell did you end up here, Hawke?"

"He called Zane when that SoHo property exploded," Vander said. "When we told him you guys were in trouble, he wanted in. Provided the gear and the helo."

Mav lifted his chin. "You have my gratitude."

Killian nodded.

"Thank you, thank you." His mother hurried over.

She hugged Killian, Ace, and then, ignoring the fact that Vander was a badass, Mav's mother charged up and hugged him too.

Luckily, Vander came from an Italian-American family. His mom and Mav's mom would be best friends, if they lived closer. Vander hugged her back.

"Remi?" Mav asked.

Vander nodded to a curtain.

Mav hobbled over, towing his bag on wheels, and pulled the curtain back. Love for his friends hit him.

Remi sat on the bed. Liam sat beside her, saying something that made her laugh. Zane was on her other side, holding her hand.

Aspen and Monroe were wiping her arms and face.

Her head turned.

And he saw it.

Something he'd never seen in a woman's eyes before —love. He'd seen lust, desire, want, envy, but in Remi's eyes he saw love, trust, and forever.

She leaped off the bed and ran to him.

He caught her, holding her tight. His side pulled, but he didn't care.

"Remi." Mav's mother hustled forward, and hugged her.

Remi hesitated a second, then hugged her back.

"What the hell happened?" Mav's brother, Carlos, demanded.

"It's a long story." Mav claimed Remi again and looked at Vander.

"The assassin is in police custody and facing some significant charges," Vander said.

"Assassin?" Mav's mom whispered.

"It's over, Mom."

She nodded and leaned into Mav's father.

"It's over. We're all safe," Remi said.

Mav stroked his thumb along her cheekbone. "Yes, we are." But some things were just beginning. "Remi—"

"Where is my girl?" another loud, female voice demanded.

Mav looked up. Boone was leading Mama Alma in.

And the rest of Remi's family were behind them.

They poured into the examination room.

There was noise, tears, hugging. Some nurses finally hustled them into a private waiting room.

Mav was ordered back to bed, which he ignored. Instead, he found a chair and pulled Remi into his lap.

She looked exhausted. They'd both been hugged and kissed within inches of their lives.

"Ruben and Tisdale?" she asked.

"Stable. They should make full recoveries."

She released a breath. "Good."

Mav pulled out his phone and tapped. He heard the ping of her phone.

She read the text and smiled.

His phone pinged.

I love you, too.

Mav typed again.

This time, her eyes widened. She frowned and typed.

You just asked me to marry you via text?

"Do you need something else?" he asked.

Her eyes narrowed.

He touched his phone again, activating a program that he had on there.

A second later, her phone played a song. It was "Marry You", by Bruno Mars. He heard her gasp.

"Oh, my God, did you just hack my phone?" she asked.

"Yes."

She tapped on it. "I'm going to hack you back, Rivera."

He hoped so. "You've already stolen my most heavily guarded possession. My heart."

Her face softened. "Damn, don't make me cry." She sniffed. "And the answer will be yes, after you ask me again when we aren't in scrubs, smeared with blood, and surrounded by a million people."

Elation filled him. "Deal."

He covered her mouth with his.

Remi

Dancing to a new pop song, I leaned forward and finished my makeup in the mirror.

I would still be very happy to live in Mav's master bathroom. I grinned at myself in the mirror. But instead of his bathroom, I was living in his whole place.

I was living with Mav.

Swaying my hips to the beat, I took a second to admire my short, tight Herve Leger dress. To say it hugged my curves was an understatement.

It was electric blue, which I'd learned was Mav's favorite color, and it left one shoulder bare.

I looked hot.

Finishing with my makeup, I fluffed my hair. I left it out, artfully tousled. I had diamond studs in my ears. He'd given them to me for our one-week anniversary.

I'd given him a mug, which he loved. He had his coffee in it every day.

I strode toward the kitchen, sidestepping my clothes from last night. I'd left them dropped on the bedroom floor. Mav didn't seem to mind that I wasn't exactly the tidiest person.

My makeup was strewn through the bathroom, my clothes packed untidily into his closet.

For a man who'd avoided relationships all his life, he was a good boyfriend.

I was going to marry him one day.

We hadn't made it official, deciding to take our time and savor every moment. Plus let all the media hubbub die down after the whole hacking/The Shadow/assassination attempt drama. I could barely leave Mav's place without a crowd of paparazzi following me.

Warmth bloomed. I would marry a man who drove me crazy, loved me, got me, was sexy, grumpy, and hot.

I gave a giddy little shiver.

Now, where was he?

"Big guy," I called out, walking down the stairs. "Time to get moving, or we'll be late to Zane and Monroe's party."

I waltzed into the kitchen. *Where was my—? There.*

I found my bag and pulled out my phone. I took a second to admire the sexy Rivera Tech design. I didn't need my bag tonight, so I would just put my phone into Mav's pocket. I skimmed my hands over my dress. There was no room in this outfit.

I checked my messages. I had a text from Mama.

She'd included a photo of her smiling from her hospital bed, her room packed with flowers.

The surgery had gone well, and the doctors were optimistic. My gorgeous man had filled Mama's room with flowers of all shapes and sizes. I'd spent the day with her today, until she'd kicked me out. I'd also visited Steve and the kids, who were staying in a rental house that Mav had arranged for them until Mama's house could be repaired.

"I'm ready." Mav strode in, looking rugged and scrumptious in a charcoal suit. He had a mug in his hand. "I don't know why Zane wants to have a party."

I rolled my eyes. "There is this wild concept called fun, big guy."

He set his favorite mug on the island. It said Best Billionaire Boyfriend. He loved it.

His gaze lifted and he went so still that it looked like he'd stopped breathing.

I saw the flames ignite in his dark gaze.

Oh, boy, that gave me a little thrill. I cocked my hip. "You like my dress?"

He made a noise and stalked toward me.

I held up a hand. "We have a party to get to, remember?"

"I don't care." He gripped my hips and backed me up.

Then his mouth was on mine.

Mmm. My brain happily short-circuited.

I kissed him back and thought briefly of how long it would take to repair my makeup after a quickie.

"What's under this dress?" Mav drawled.

I bit my lip. "Rivera, have you seen how tight this dress is? There is nothing under here."

He growled, his hand slipping under the hem.

I caught his wrist. "No. Party. Friends. Family." The last word gave me a jolt. "The families will be there." I was not turning up late with sex glow and sex hair. I wouldn't be able to look Mrs. Rivera in the eye.

Mav gave an unhappy grumble. "Let's get your coat. The quicker we go, the quicker we come back, and the quicker I can peel you out of that dress."

"Deal."

We arrived at the super-skinny skyscraper with a killer view of Central Park, where Zane had a breathtaking triplex penthouse somewhere near the top.

Here I was, barely batting an eye at hanging out in a multi-million-dollar penthouse on Billionaire Row.

Barely.

In the elevator, Mav attempted to slide a hand under my dress again. I stepped out, batting at his hand and laughing.

Music played and there were people all over the classy place.

Oh, and that view. The park was draped in night shadows, the city a field of lights around it.

"Remi." Monroe strode toward us in a killer purple dress—it was fitted to her long, slim body, with tiny cap sleeves. The color was perfect with her black hair.

We hugged. We'd gotten together a couple of times. I officially loved Monroe and Aspen. They were friendly, real, kind. My sort of people.

"Most guests are up on the terrace. There's another bar up there. Zane went all out."

I nabbed a glass of champagne. "What are we celebrating?"

Monroe smiled. "Life. Love." She leaned in. "I don't know. Billionaires seem to go to a lot of parties."

I laughed. "I know. Mav hates them, but there's always a party, a dinner, or a gala."

Beside me, Mav grunted.

"Zane bought a couple of bottles of scotch that he's all excited about."

"Oh, yeah." Mav brightened. "What did he get?"

Monroe waved a hand. "I don't know. A bottle of the Macallan M."

"Nice," Mav said.

"And a bottle of Macallan Fine and Rare 60-Year-Old."

Mav made a choking sound. "I need to go and find him." He gave me a distracted kiss and shot off like a man on a mission.

"Must be some scotch," I muttered.

"Cheers." Monroe clinked her glass to mine. "Your brother's around, herding the kids. Aspen's sisters are helping him."

I scanned the party, spying Mav's family. I also noted Killian chatting with Rollo.

"Remi!"

Kaylee shot like a bullet and slammed into my legs. "KayKay. You look so pretty."

My niece was wearing a blue princess dress.

"Mama's sick," Kaylee said, face serious.

"I know, but I saw her today. She was surrounded by flowers, and feeling really good." I tapped the little girl's nose. "She's missing you."

"Really?"

"Really."

"There you are." One of Aspen's tall, blonde, athletic sisters appeared. I had no idea which one she was. "How about a drink, Kaylee?"

"A pink one?" Kaylee asked hopefully.

"That can be arranged."

Except for Mama, all my people were here. My family. My gaze moved over to Zane, Liam, and Mav. The three of them were unsurprisingly cradling heavy crystal glasses filled with amber liquid.

New friends.

And the love of my life.

Mav's head turned and he smiled at me.

Ah, I never got tired of that smile.

His mouth moved. *I love you.*

I smiled, filled with love. *I love you too*, I mouthed back.

Mav

Mav was actually enjoying this party.

He stood up on the terrace now. It was cold, but Zane had braziers set up everywhere to ward off the chill.

There were also fairy lights strung up, and they made the place look nice. Remi had called it pretty and magical.

There was music playing, and some people were dancing. Remi was dancing with Kaylee. Aspen's sisters were cutting some wild moves. Monroe was dancing with her brother, Maguire, and Rollo. He saw Aspen head off the dance floor toward a chair. She looked pale, and Liam said she'd come down with something.

"Good party." Vander stepped up beside Mav, beer in hand.

"Yeah. I heard you're heading back to San Francisco tomorrow."

"Yes. The job here is all wrapped up." Vander's dark-blue gaze moved to Ace, who was frowning and tapping on his phone. "Ace is edgy to get home."

Mav studied Ace's lean face. "Woman problems?"

Vander arched a dark brow. "He's not saying, but my best guess is yes. Which is interesting, as he doesn't usually have woman problems." Vander sipped his beer. "Seems the best idea is to steer clear."

"I thought that way." Mav looked at Remi. "I had a bad relationship once, and I did my best to avoid any entanglements after." Mav smiled. "Then Remi crashed into my world and tipped it upside down."

"I like my world right-side-up, thanks," Vander said.

Mav tipped his drink to Vander. "Your brothers are both in love. And your best friend. One day, some woman is going to shatter that control you like so much."

Vander scowled and shook his head.

"And you'll fight the world for her. To make her smile, to keep her happy, to keep her safe, to make her yours."

Vander just sipped his beer and looked unconvinced.

"Any news on The Shadow?" Mav asked, figuring by Vander's expression it was time to change the subject.

"Felix Garcia, aka Leven Shen, aka Bronson Roberts, aka a whole bunch of aliases. He's been whisked away by government agents. A lot of agencies from various countries around the world would like to get their hands on him. They've linked him to some murders, and some other ugly crimes. He'll never see the light of day."

"Good."

"Rayner and a few other people The Shadow had contact with were brought in for questioning. Didn't know anything. They were just convenient dupes when

The Shadow needed lackeys." Vander's phone rang. "Excuse me, I've got to take this."

"Sure."

Ace wandered over, still scowling at his phone.

Mav eyed Vander's tech man. "Problem?"

"Just someone who isn't returning my calls."

"What did you do to piss her off?" Mav asked.

Ace's scowl deepened. "We... Had a thing. She's been avoiding me ever since."

"Ah."

"She works for Norcross Security." Ace blew out a breath.

Which had to make things sticky. Mav glanced over at Vander, who was still talking on the phone. "Ah," he repeated, knowingly.

"We'll be back in San Francisco tomorrow. I'm going to find her and work this out."

He sounded like a man on a mission.

Vander returned. "Ace, change of plans."

"What?" Ace asked unhappily.

"We just got a big cybersecurity job in New Orleans. Two weeks of work. I need you there tomorrow. I'll get your flights changed so you can fly straight there."

Mav watched the struggle of emotions on Ace's face.

"You have a problem with that?" Vander asked.

"No." Ace gulped more of his beer. "No problem."

The clinking sound of silverware tapping on glass interrupted their conversation.

Zane stepped into the center of the space and the music stopped.

"Thanks for coming. It's so wonderful you're here to help Monroe and I celebrate. We've had a lot of upheaval lately. Thieves, bombs—" he glanced toward Liam "—blackmail, kidnapping—" he met Mav's gaze "—hackers and assassins."

There was a smattering of laughter.

"But my friends and I have so much to celebrate. For a long time, we just celebrated our business successes, but falling in love with an amazing woman has made me appreciate so much more. My family." He nodded at his mother. "My friends." He lifted the glass to Liam and Mav. "And the love of my life. Come here, Wildcat."

Smiling, Monroe came forward, love all over her face.

There was a wolf whistle from a curly-haired blonde in the crowd—Monroe's best friend, Sabrina.

"I have something for you, Monroe," Zane said.

She turned to the crowd and rolled her eyes. "The man is always buying me shiny baubles."

"The gall of him," Remi called out.

More laughter.

"I do have something shiny for you," Zane said.

Mav sucked in a breath.

"Roth—" Monroe turned back to Zane, and saw him on one knee before her, a small box in his hand. She froze.

"Monroe O'Connor. I love you. You bring so much color to my life. You see *me*. You love me. And I can't live without you."

"Zane," a quiet whisper.

"Marry me?"

She opened her mouth, but no words came out.

Zane cocked his head. "If you want, I can put it in the safe and let you crack it open."

She blushed as the crowd hooted and whistled.

"Make me the happiest man in the world?" Zane asked.

"Yes." Tears rolled down her cheeks, but she was smiling. "Absolutely, yes."

Damn. Mav's best friend was getting married.

He watched Zane scoop up Monroe and kiss her, with New York spread out and glittering behind them.

Remi burrowed into Mav's side and sighed. "So romantic."

"Aspen!" one of Aspen's sisters cried.

The PI stumbled, then crumpled like a wet tissue.

In a superhuman move, Liam made it to her side and caught her in his arms before she hit the floor.

"Darling, that's it. I'm calling the doctor. No more arguments."

"God, no, I'm okay." Aspen straightened. "And the doctor can't help."

He looked panicked. "What? What's wrong?"

Aspen bit her lip. "*God.*"

"Aspen—"

"I wasn't going to say anything yet, but... Liam, I'm pregnant."

Silence.

Liam did an excellent impersonation of a statue.

Aspen gave a watery smile. "I just took the test today. It's really early. I don't know how it happened. Well, I do know, but—"

Liam cupped her cheeks. "We're having a baby?"

Aspen bit her lip. "It's sudden. Too soon—"

"No, it's ours. And it's perfect." He kissed her.

Aspen melted into him and kissed him back.

The crowd broke out in applause and cheers.

"Wowser," Remi said with a sniff. "Two out of three. Do you have any big announcements?"

He smiled. He had the ring at home. A funky design filled with sapphires and diamonds. "Not tonight." But soon.

"You billionaires sure know how to throw a party," an older woman said. She had an evil-looking white cat clutched in her arms.

It was Mrs. Kerber, Aspen's elderly neighbor. The cat gave Mav a flat stare, and he got the uncanny feeling it was plotting his murder.

Mav pulled Remi to the railing.

He saw that Zane and Monroe were slow dancing. Liam was holding Aspen against him like she was a rare prize, a hand over her belly, and love in his eyes. Aspen's mother and sisters were with them, crying happy tears.

"I want that," Remi whispered. "Love, marriage, kids. I want to make a home."

Like she hadn't had until Mama had given her one.

"Sounds like a good plan." Just weeks ago, it would've sounded like hell to him.

Now, it sounded like heaven.

Remi gave him a saucy look. "Now, I just need to find the right man."

Mav grabbed her and lifted her off her feet. "No man, just me."

"Just you." She smiled at him.

"And soon it will be your turn to get a ring. So be prepared."

"I'm always prepared, big guy. I'm a hacker, remember."

His hacker. His angel.

He kissed her under the lights, in the middle of the crowd of friends and family. Ready for the life they'd make together.

I hope you enjoyed Remi and Mav's story!

Want to know more about Vander Norcross? Then check out the first book in the Norcross Security series, *The Investigator*, starring Vander's brother Rhys. **Read on for a preview of the first chapter.**

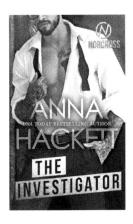

Don't miss out! For updates about new releases, free books, and other fun stuff, sign up for my VIP mailing list and get your *free box set* containing three action-packed romances.

Visit here to get started: <u>www.annahackett.com</u>

Would you like
a FREE BOX SET
of my books?

PREVIEW: THE INVESTIGATOR

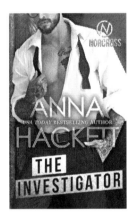

There was a glass of chardonnay with her name on it waiting for her at home.

Haven McKinney smiled. The museum was closed, and she was *done* for the day.

As she walked across the East gallery of the Hutton Museum, her heels clicked on the marble floor.

God, she loved the place. The creamy marble that made up the flooring and wrapped around the grand pillars was gorgeous. It had that hushed air of grandeur that made her heart squeeze a little every time she stepped inside. But more than that, the amazing art the Hutton housed sang to the art lover in her blood.

Snagging a job here as the curator six months ago had been a dream come true. She'd been at a low point in her life. Very low. Haven swallowed a snort and circled a stunning white-marble sculpture of a naked, reclining woman with the most perfect resting bitch face. She'd never guessed that her life would come crashing down at age twenty-nine.

She lifted her chin. Miami was her past. The Hutton and San Francisco were her future. No more throwing caution to the wind. She had a plan, and she was sticking to it.

She paused in front of a stunning exhibit of traditional Chinese painting and calligraphy. It was one of their newer exhibits, and had been Haven's brainchild. Nearby, an interactive display was partially assembled. Over the next few days, her staff would finish the installation. Excitement zipped through Haven. She couldn't wait to have the touchscreens operational. It was her passion to make art more accessible, especially to children. To help them be a part of it, not just look at it. To learn, to feel, to enjoy.

Art had helped her through some of the toughest times in her life, and she wanted to share that with others.

She looked at the gorgeous old paintings again. One portrayed a mountainous landscape with beautiful maple trees. It soothed her nerves.

Wine would soothe her nerves, as well. *Right*. She

needed to get upstairs to her office and grab her handbag, then get an Uber home.

Her cell phone rang and she unclipped it from the lanyard she wore at the museum. "Hello?"

"Change of plans, girlfriend," a smoky female voice said. "Let's go out and celebrate being gorgeous, successful, and single. I'm done at the office, and believe me, it has been a *grueling* day."

Haven smiled at her new best friend. She'd met Gia Norcross when she joined the Hutton. Gia's wealthy brother, Easton Norcross, owned the museum, and was Haven's boss. The museum was just a small asset in the businessman's empire. Haven suspected Easton owned at least a third of San Francisco. Maybe half.

She liked and respected her boss. Easton could be tough, but he valued her opinions. And she loved his bossy, take-charge, energetic sister. Gia ran a highly successful PR firm in the city, and did all the PR and advertising for the Hutton. They'd met not long after Haven had started work at the museum.

After their first meeting, Gia had dragged Haven out to her favorite restaurant and bar, and the rest was history.

"I guess making people's Instagram look pretty and not staged is hard work," Haven said with a grin.

"Bitch." Gia laughed. "God, I had a meeting with a businessman caught in...well, let's just say he and his assistant were *not* taking notes on the boardroom table."

Haven felt an old, unwelcome memory rise up. She mentally stomped it down. "I don't feel sorry for the cheating asshole, I feel sorry for whatever poor shmuck got more than they were paid for when they walked into the boardroom."

"Actually, it was the cheating businessman's wife."

"Uh-oh."

"And the assistant was male," Gia added.

"Double uh-oh."

"Then said cheater comes to my PR firm, telling me to clean up his mess, because he's thinking he might run for governor one day. I mean, I'm good, but I can't wrangle miracles."

Haven suspected that Gia had verbally eviscerated the man and sent him on his way. Gia Norcross had a sharp tongue, and wasn't afraid to use it.

"So, grueling day and I need alcohol. I'll meet you at ONE65, and the first drink is on me."

"I'm pretty wiped, Gia—"

"Uh-uh, no excuses. I'll see you in an hour." And with that, Gia was gone.

Haven clipped her phone to her lanyard. Well, it looked like she was having that chardonnay at ONE65, the six-story, French dining experience Gia loved. Each level offered something different, from patisserie, to bistro and grill, to bar and lounge.

Haven walked into the museum's main gallery, and her blood pressure dropped to a more normal level. It was her favorite space in the museum. The smell of wood, the gorgeous lights gleaming overhead, and the amazing paintings combined to create a soothing room. She smoothed her hands down her fitted, black skirt. Haven was tall, at five foot eight, and curvy, just like her mom had been. Her boobs, currently covered by a cute, white blouse with a tie around her neck, weren't much to write home about, but she had to buy her skirts one size bigger. She sighed. No matter how much she walked or jogged —*blergh*, okay, she didn't jog much—she still had an ass.

Even in her last couple of months in Miami, when stress had caused her to lose a bunch of weight due to everything going on, her ass hadn't budged.

Memories of Miami—and her douchebag-of-epic-proportions-ex—threatened, churning like storm clouds on the horizon.

Nope. She locked those thoughts down. She was *not* going there.

She had a plan, and the number one thing for taking back and rebuilding her life was *no* men. She'd sworn off anyone with a Y chromosome.

She didn't need one, didn't want one, she was D-O-N-E, done.

She stopped in front of the museum's star attraction. Claude Monet's *Water Lilies*.

Haven loved the impressionist's work. She loved the colors, the delicate strokes. This one depicted water lilies and lily pads floating on a gentle pond. His paintings always made an impact, and had a haunting, yet soothing feel to them.

It was also worth just over a hundred million dollars.

The price tag still made her heart flutter. She'd put a business case to Easton, and they'd purchased the painting three weeks ago at auction. Haven had planned out the display down to the rivets used on the wood. She'd thrown herself into the project.

Gia had put together a killer marketing campaign,

and Haven had reluctantly been interviewed by the local paper. But it had paid off. Ticket sales to the museum were up, and everyone wanted to see *Water Lilies*.

Footsteps echoed through the empty museum, and she turned to see a uniformed security guard appear in the doorway.

"Ms. McKinney?"

"Yes, David? I was just getting ready to leave."

"Sorry to delay you. There's a delivery truck at the back entrance. They say they have a delivery of a Zadkine bronze."

Haven frowned, running through the next day's schedule in her head. "That's due tomorrow."

"It sounds like they had some other deliveries nearby and thought they'd squeeze it in."

She glanced at her slim, silver wristwatch, fighting back annoyance. She'd had a long day, and now she'd be late to meet Gia. "Fine. Have them bring it in."

With a nod, David disappeared. Haven pulled out her phone and quickly fired off a text to warn Gia that she'd be late. Then Haven headed up to her office, and checked her notes for tomorrow. She had several calls to make to chase down some pieces for a new exhibit she wanted to launch in the winter. There were some restoration quotes to go over, and a charity gala for her art charity to plan. She needed to get down into the storage rooms and see if there was anything they could cycle out and put on display.

God, she loved her job. Not many people would get excited about digging around in dusty storage rooms, but Haven couldn't wait.

She made sure her laptop was off and grabbed her handbag. She slipped her lanyard off and stuffed her phone in her bag.

When she reached the bottom of the stairs, she heard a strange noise from the gallery. A muffled pop, then a thump.

Frowning, she took one step toward the gallery.

Suddenly, David staggered through the doorway, a splotch of red on his shirt.

Haven's pulse spiked. *Oh God, was that blood?* "David—"

"Run." He collapsed to the floor.

Fear choking her, she kicked off her heels and spun. She had to get help.

But she'd only taken two steps when a hand sank into her hair, pulling her neat twist loose, and sending her brown hair cascading over her shoulders.

"Let me go!"

She was dragged into the main gallery, and when she lifted her head, her gut churned.

Five men dressed in black, all wearing balaclavas, stood in a small group.

No...oh, no.

Their other guard, Gus, stood with his hands in the air. He was older, former military. She was shoved closer toward him.

"Ms. McKinney, you okay?" Gus asked.

She managed a nod. "They shot David."

"I kn—"

"No talking," one man growled.

Haven lifted her chin. "What do you want?" There was a slight quaver in her voice.

The man who'd grabbed her glared. His cold, blue eyes glittered through the slits in his balaclava. Then he ignored her, and with the others, they turned to face the *Water Lilies*.

Haven's stomach dropped. *No.* This couldn't be happening.

A thin man moved forward, studying the painting's gilt frame with gloved hands. "It's wired to an alarm."

Blue Eyes, clearly the group's leader, turned and aimed the gun at Gus' barrel chest. "Disconnect it."

"No," the guard said belligerently.

"I'm not asking."

Haven held up her hands. "Please—"

The gun fired. Gus dropped to one knee, pressing a hand to his shoulder.

"No!" she cried.

The leader stepped forward and pressed the gun to the older man's head.

"No." Haven fought back her fear and panic. "Don't hurt him. I'll disconnect it."

Slowly, she inched toward the painting, carefully avoiding the thin man still standing close to it. She touched the security panel built in beside the frame, pressing her palm to the small pad.

A second later, there was a discreet beep.

Two other men came forward and grabbed the frame.

She glanced around at them. "You're making a mistake. If you know who owns this museum, then you know you won't get away with this." Who would go up against the Norcross family? Easton, rich as sin, had a lot of connections, but his brother, Vander... Haven suppressed a shiver. Gia's middle brother might be hot, but he scared the bejesus out of Haven.

Vander Norcross, former military badass, owned Norcross Security and Investigations. His team had put in the high-tech security for the museum.

No one in their right mind wanted to go up against Vander, or the third Norcross brother who also worked with Vander, or the rest of Vander's team of badasses.

"Look, if you just—"

The blow to her head made her stagger. She blinked, pain radiating through her face. Blue Eyes had back-handed her.

He moved in and hit her again, and Haven cried out, clutching her face. It wasn't the first time she'd been hit. Her douchebag ex had hit her once. That was the day she'd left him for good.

But this was worse. Way worse.

"Shut up, you stupid bitch."

The next blow sent her to the floor. She thought she heard someone chuckle. He followed with a kick to her ribs, and Haven curled into a ball, a sob in her throat.

Her vision wavered and she blinked. Blue Eyes crouched down, putting his hand to the tiles right in front of her. Dizziness hit her, and she vaguely took in the freckles on the man's hand. They formed a spiral pattern.

"No one talks back to me," the man growled. "Especially a woman." He moved away.

She saw the men were busy maneuvering the painting off the wall. It was easy for two people to move.

She knew its exact dimensions—eighty by one hundred centimeters.

No one was paying any attention to her. Fighting through the nausea and dizziness, she dragged herself a few inches across the floor, closer to the nearby pillar. A pillar that had one of several hidden, high-tech panic buttons built into it.

When the men were turned away, she reached up and pressed the button.

Then blackness sucked her under.

HAVEN SAT on one of the lovely wooden benches she'd had installed around the museum. She'd wanted somewhere for guests to sit and take in the art.

She'd never expected to be sitting on one, holding a melting ice pack to her throbbing face, and staring at the empty wall where a multi-million-dollar masterpiece should be hanging. And she definitely didn't expect to be doing it with police dusting black powder all over the museum's walls.

Tears pricked her eyes. She was alive, her guards were hurt but alive, and that was what mattered. The police had questioned her and she'd told them everything she could remember. The paramedics had checked her over and given her the ice pack. Nothing was broken, but she'd been told to expect swelling and bruising.

David and Gus had been taken to the hospital. She'd been assured the men would be okay. Last she'd heard, David was in surgery. Her throat tightened. *Oh, God.*

What was she going to tell Easton?

Haven bit her lip and a tear fell down her cheek. She hadn't cried in months. She'd shed more than enough tears over Leo after he'd gone crazy and hit her. She'd left Miami the next day. She'd needed to get away from her ex and, unfortunately, despite loving her job at a classy Miami art gallery, Leo's cousin had owned it. Alyssa had been the one who had introduced them.

Haven had learned a painful lesson to not mix business and pleasure.

She'd been done with Leo's growing moodiness, outbursts, and cheating on her and hitting her had been the last straw. *Asshole.*

She wiped the tear away. San Francisco was as far from Miami as she could get and still be in the continental US. This was supposed to be her fresh new start.

She heard footsteps—solid, quick, and purposeful. Easton strode in.

He was a tall man, with dark hair that curled at the collar of his perfectly fitted suit. Haven had sworn off men, but she was still woman enough to appreciate her boss' good looks. His mother was Italian-American, and she'd passed down her very good genes to her children.

Like his brothers, Easton had been in the military, too, although he'd joined the Army Rangers. It showed in his muscled body. Once, she'd seen his shirt sleeves rolled up when they'd had a late meeting. He had some interesting ink that was totally at odds with his sophisticated-businessman persona.

His gaze swept the room, his jaw tight. It settled on her and he strode over.

"Haven—"

"Oh God, Easton. I'm so sorry."

He sat beside her and took her free hand. He squeezed her cold fingers, then he looked at her face and cursed.

She hadn't been brave enough to look in the mirror, but she guessed it was bad.

"They took the *Water Lilies*," she said.

"Okay, don't worry about it just now."

She gave a hiccupping laugh. "Don't worry? It's worth a hundred and ten *million* dollars."

A muscle ticked in his jaw. "You're okay, and that's the main thing. And the guards are in serious but stable condition at the hospital."

She nodded numbly. "It's all my fault."

Easton's gaze went to the police, and then moved back to her. "That's not true."

"I let them in." Her voice broke. God, she wanted the marble floor to crack and swallow her.

"Don't worry." Easton's face turned very serious. "Vander and Rhys will find the painting."

Her boss' tone made her shiver. Something made her suspect that Easton wanted his brothers to find the men who'd stolen the painting more than recovering the priceless piece of art.

She licked her lips, and felt the skin on her cheek tug. She'd have some spectacular bruises later. *Great. Thanks, universe.*

Then Easton's head jerked up, and Haven followed his gaze.

A man stood in the doorway. She hadn't heard him

coming. Nope, Vander Norcross moved silently, like a ghost.

He was a few inches over six feet, had a powerful body, and radiated authority. His suit didn't do much to tone down the sense that a predator had stalked into the room. While Easton was handsome, Vander wasn't. His face was too rugged, and while both he and Easton had blue eyes, Vander's were dark indigo, and as cold as the deepest ocean depths.

He didn't look happy. She fought back a shiver.

Then another man stepped up beside Vander.

Haven's chest locked. *Oh, no. No, no, no.*

She should have known. He was Vander's top investigator. Rhys Matteo Norcross, the youngest of the Norcross brothers.

At first glance, he looked like his brothers—similar build, muscular body, dark hair and bronze skin. But Rhys was the youngest, and he had a charming edge his brothers didn't share. He smiled more frequently, and his shaggy, thick hair always made her imagine him as a rock star, holding a guitar and making girls scream.

Haven was also totally, one hundred percent in lust with him. Any time he got near, he made her body flare to life, her heart beat faster, and made her brain freeze up. She could barely talk around the man.

She did *not* want Rhys Norcross to notice her. Or talk to her. Or turn his soulful, brown eyes her way.

Nuh-uh. No way. She'd sworn off men. This one should have a giant warning sign hanging on him. *Watch out, heartbreak waiting to happen.*

Rhys had been in the military with Vander. Some

hush-hush special unit that no one talked about. Now he worked at Norcross Security—apparently finding anything and anyone.

He also raced cars and boats in his free time. The man liked to go fast. Oh, and he bedded women. His reputation was legendary. Rhys liked a variety of adventures and experiences.

It was lucky Haven had sworn off men.

Especially when they happened to be her boss' brother.

And especially, especially when they were also her best friend's brother.

Off limits.

She saw the pair turn to look her and Easton's way.

Crap. Pulse racing, she looked at her bare feet and red toenails, which made her realize she hadn't recovered her shoes yet. They were her favorites.

She felt the men looking at her, and like she was drawn by a magnet, she looked up. Vander was scowling. Rhys' dark gaze was locked on her.

Haven's traitorous heart did a little tango in her chest.

Before she knew what was happening, Rhys went down on one knee in front of her.

She saw rage twist his handsome features. Then he shocked her by cupping her jaw, and pushing the ice pack away.

They'd never talked much. At Gia's parties, Haven purposely avoided him. He'd never touched her before, and she felt the warmth of him singe through her.

His eyes flashed. "It's going to be okay, baby."

Baby?

He stroked her cheekbone, those long fingers gentle.

Fighting for some control, Haven closed her hand over his wrist. She swallowed. "I—"

"Don't worry, Haven. I'm going to find the man who did this to you and make him regret it."

Her belly tightened. *Oh, God.* When was the last time anyone had looked out for her like this? She was certain no one had ever promised to hunt anyone down for her. Her gaze dropped to his lips.

He had amazingly shaped lips, a little fuller than such a tough man should have, framed by dark stubble.

There was a shift in his eyes and his face warmed. His fingers kept stroking her skin and she felt that caress all over.

Then she heard the click of heels moving at speed. Gia burst into the room.

"What the hell is going on?"

Haven jerked back from Rhys and his hypnotic touch. Damn, she'd been proven right—she was so weak where this man was concerned.

Gia hurried toward them. She was five-foot-four, with a curvy, little body, and a mass of dark, curly hair. As usual, she wore one of her power suits—short skirt, fitted jacket, and sky-high heels.

"Out of my way." Gia shouldered Rhys aside. When her friend got a look at Haven, her mouth twisted. "I'm going to *kill* them."

"Gia," Vander said. "The place is filled with cops. Maybe keep your plans for murder and vengeance quiet."

"Fix this." She pointed at Vander's chest, then at

Rhys. Then she turned and hugged Haven. "You're coming home with me."

"Gia—"

"No. No arguments." Gia held up her palm like a traffic cop. Haven had seen "the hand" before. It was pointless arguing.

Besides, she realized she didn't want to be alone. And the quicker she got away from Rhys' dark, far-too-perceptive gaze, the better.

Norcross Security

The Investigator
The Troubleshooter
The Specialist
The Bodyguard

PREVIEW: TEAM 52 AND THS

Want to learn more about the mysterious, covert *Team 52*? Check out the first book in the series, *Mission: Her Protection.*

When Rowan's Arctic research team pulls a strange object out of the ice in Northern

Canada, things start to go wrong...very, very wrong. Rescued by a covert, black ops team, she finds herself in the powerful arms of a man with scary gold eyes. A man who vows to do everything and anything to protect her...

Dr. Rowan Schafer has learned it's best to do things herself and not depend on anyone else. Her cold, academic parents taught her that lesson. She loves the challenge of running a research base, until the day her scientists discover the object in a retreating glacier. Under attack, Rowan finds herself fighting to survive... until the mysterious Team 52 arrives.

Former special forces Marine Lachlan Hunter's military career ended in blood and screams, until he was recruited to lead a special team. A team tasked with a top-secret mission—to secure and safeguard pieces of powerful ancient technology. Married to his job, he's done too much and seen too much to risk inflicting his demons on a woman. But when his team arrives in the Arctic, he uncovers both an unexplained artifact, and a young girl from his past, now all grown up. A woman who ignites emotions inside him like never before.

But as Team 52 heads back to their base in Nevada, other hostile forces are after the artifact. Rowan finds herself under attack, and as the bullets fly, Lachlan vows to protect her at all costs. But in the face of danger like they've never seen before, will it be enough to keep her alive.

Team 52
Mission: Her Protection
Mission: Her Rescue
Mission: Her Security
Mission: Her Defense
Mission: Her Safety
Mission: Her Freedom
Mission: Her Shield
Also Available as Audiobooks!

Want to learn more about *Treasure Hunter Security*? Check out the first book in the series, *Undiscovered*, Declan Ward's action-packed story.

One former Navy SEAL. One dedicated archeologist. One secret map to a fabulous lost oasis.

Finding undiscovered treasures is always daring, dangerous, and deadly. Perfect for the men of Treasure Hunter Security. Former Navy SEAL Declan Ward is haunted by the demons of his past and throws everything he has into his security business—Treasure Hunter Security. Dangerous archeological digs – no problem. Daring expeditions – sure thing. Museum security for invaluable exhibits – easy. But on a simple dig in the Egyptian desert, he collides with a stubborn, smart archeologist, Dr. Layne Rush, and together they get swept into a deadly treasure hunt for a mythical lost oasis. When an evil from his past reappears, Declan vows to do anything to protect Layne.

Dr. Layne Rush is dedicated to building a successful career—a promise to the parents she lost far too young. But when her dig is plagued by strange accidents, targeted by a lethal black market antiquities ring, and artifacts are stolen, she is forced to turn to Treasure Hunter Security, and to the tough, sexy, and too-used-to-giving-orders Declan. Soon her organized dig morphs into a wild treasure hunt across the desert dunes.

Danger is hunting them every step of the way, and Layne and Declan must find a way to work together...to not only find the treasure but to survive.

Treasure Hunter Security
Undiscovered
Uncharted
Unexplored
Unfathomed

Untraveled
Unmapped
Unidentified
Undetected
Also Available as Audiobooks!

Treasure Hunter Security

Undiscovered

Uncharted

Unexplored

Unfathomed

Untraveled

Unmapped

Unidentified

Undetected

Also Available as Audiobooks!

Eon Warriors

Edge of Eon

Touch of Eon

Heart of Eon

Kiss of Eon

Mark of Eon

Claim of Eon

Storm of Eon

Soul of Eon

Also Available as Audiobooks!

Galactic Gladiators: House of Rone

Sentinel

Defender

Centurion

Paladin

Guard

Weapons Master

Also Available as Audiobooks!

Galactic Gladiators

Gladiator

Warrior

Hero

Protector

Champion

Barbarian

Beast

Rogue

Guardian

Cyborg

Imperator

Hunter

Also Available as Audiobooks!

Hell Squad

Marcus

Cruz

Gabe

Reed

Roth

Noah

Shaw

Holmes

Niko

Finn

Devlin

Theron

Hemi

Ash

Levi

Manu

Griff

Dom

Survivors

Tane

Also Available as Audiobooks!

The Anomaly Series

Time Thief

Mind Raider

Soul Stealer

Salvation

Anomaly Series Box Set

The Phoenix Adventures

Among Galactic Ruins

At Star's End

In the Devil's Nebula

On a Rogue Planet

Beneath a Trojan Moon

Beyond Galaxy's Edge

On a Cyborg Planet

Return to Dark Earth

On a Barbarian World

Lost in Barbarian Space

Through Uncharted Space

Crashed on an Ice World

Perma Series

Winter Fusion

A Galactic Holiday

Warriors of the Wind

Tempest

Storm & Seduction

Fury & Darkness

Standalone Titles

Savage Dragon

Hunter's Surrender

One Night with the Wolf

For more information visit www.annahackett.com

ABOUT THE AUTHOR

I'm a USA Today bestselling romance author who's passionate about ***fast-paced***, ***emotion-filled*** contemporary and science fiction romance. I love writing about people overcoming unbeatable odds and achieving seemingly impossible goals. I like to believe it's possible for all of us to do the same.

I live in Australia with my own personal hero and two very busy, always-on-the-move sons.

For release dates, behind-the-scenes info, free books, and other fun stuff, sign up for the latest news here:

Website: www.annahackett.com

Printed in Great Britain
by Amazon